"Stay low until I say go."

Beau began to count down.

On the last number, the trio pushed their shutters open and tossed the explosives. Evie was satisfied to hear a great boom as they all went off as one. A yelp told them one of their attackers had been hit by some flying debris. When she looked over, Beau had his Glock out and ready to fire. Evie pulled her 9 mm as well.

"Come on. They seem to be scattering. Mia, stay between us." Beau led the way to the door.

He eased it open then motioned for them to follow.

They ran for the main road, but their attackers recovered quickly. It wasn't long before more shots began to echo around them. They had to stay low as they ran as fast as they could through the thick brush covering the open pasture.

The road was just yards away, however, when the sound of a deep voice made them all stop where they were.

"Everybody stop right there!"

Sommer Smith teaches high school English and loves animals. She loves reading romances and writing about fairy tales. She started writing her first novel when she was thirteen and has wanted to write romances since. Her three children provide her inspiration to write with their many antics. With two dogs and a horse to keep her active in between, Sommer stays busy traveling to ball games and colleges in two states.

Books by Sommer Smith

Love Inspired Suspense

Under Suspicion
Attempted Abduction
Ranch Under Siege
Wyoming Cold Case Secrets
Wyoming Ranch Ambush

Visit the Author Profile page at LoveInspired.com.

WYOMING RANCH AMBUSH

SOMMER SMITH

LOVE INSPIRED® SUSPENSE
INSPIRATIONAL ROMANCE

Recycling programs for this product may not exist in your area.

ISBN-13: 978-1-335-59904-9

Wyoming Ranch Ambush

For questions and comments about the quality of this book, please contact us at CustomerService@Harlequin.com.

Love Inspired
22 Adelaide St. West, 41st Floor
Toronto, Ontario M5H 4E3, Canada
www.LoveInspired.com

Printed in U.S.A.

In God have I put my trust: I will not be afraid
what man can do unto me.

—*Psalm* 56:11

To my sweetheart. Thank you for doing everything
in your power to help me reach my deadlines.
You are a real-life hero, and you inspire me every day.

ONE

This might have been a bad idea.

Evie Langston hadn't been camping since she was twelve years old. No matter how well she thought she remembered, she wasn't doing well at setting up camp, even if it was just for one night. To make matters worse, she was starting to realize Wyoming was nothing like her former home in Oklahoma. It was cold, rocky and unfamiliar. She didn't know anyone here, and the sense of adventure was seriously starting to wear off. What had she been thinking?

"Evie, I'm cold. Are you going to make a campfire or not?" Mia looked up at her with limpid blue eyes.

All Evie wanted to do was make her little sister happy. Mia deserved some happiness in her life for a change. Poor Mia had grown up in the city under the care of a nanny for the past seven years. She was now nine years old, and Evie wanted to show her what else was out there. But apparently Evie had spent too much time living in the city these past couple of years herself. Working for a big agroceutical firm in Oklahoma City had started to overshadow her country roots. Her childhood had been spent farther east on a farm in a rural Oklahoma town where there was far more grass than concrete. But she seemed to have lost some of her survival skills along the way.

She couldn't get the fire to start.

"Mia, maybe it wasn't a good night for this. After all, we just got to Wyoming. We should just go back home for the night. The beds are made back at the ranch house." Evie tried for a light tone.

Mia wasn't buying it. "I thought you said this was going to be fun. You can't even get the fire started."

Evie took a deep breath. She hadn't had custody of her little sister for long, and sometimes she had a difficult time responding to Mia's petulance with patience. The girl had traveled a tough road for any nine-year-old. She might have been raised with a silver spoon, so to speak, but recently her father had died. It happened quite suddenly—a plane crash in which he had been taking a vacation with a girlfriend instead of his only daughter. He had left Mia wealthy, but quite alone in the world except for Evie, her half sister. Their mother had died of a rare case of pneumonia when Mia was only two years old.

"I'm trying. But I don't think our firewood has cured long enough. It seems to be a bit damp." She laughed, hoping to lighten Mia's mood.

It didn't work.

Mia crossed her skinny arms. "I don't wanna go back to the ranch house. It's old and smelly there."

Evie bit back a sharp reply. Yes, the ranch house was old, but she was going to remodel. It would just take time. She had already explained all of this to Mia, and that she had to work within a budget. The money would have to go toward the riding and rehabilitation facilities first, because that would be where she would continue to make an income.

But Mia tended to act a bit spoiled, thanks to Evie's stepfather. He had always had the means to give Mia exactly what she wanted. And he had tried to make up for the fact that a nanny took on most of her care by buying her whatever luxuries she wanted.

Evie didn't have that kind of money. Mia had money accessible through a trust fund set up by her father, Davidoff Terrano. It could be used for any large and necessary expenses, but it didn't mean Evie could provide the standard of living Mia was accustomed to. Nor was Michael Langston, Evie's father, still around to help her with her new charge. He had died in a wildfire accident when Evie was twelve, so at least she could relate to Mia's loss. They had struggled to get by for a while until Evie's mother, Annette, met and married Mia's father many years later.

Perhaps it was time Mia learned some hard lessons.

"I'm sorry, Mia, but this just isn't going to work without a campfire. It's too cold. Start packing up." Evie didn't wait for the whining argument to come but rose from where she squatted by the pile of firewood and began to pack their things.

Honestly, she had wanted to take her own mind off recent events as much as she wanted to give her sister a happy memory to begin life here in Wyoming. She had learned from a friend just that morning that her ex-boyfriend Ruark had been found dead under suspicious circumstances the night before. It had devastated her to hear it, even if she had long since lost any emotional connection to Ruark. Evie had known when they broke up that something was terribly wrong in the man's life, but she had only wanted to get away. Of course, that hadn't meant she would want anything tragic to happen to him.

With her hands on her hips and her lower lip quivering, Mia watched her start packing. She looked ready to throw a temper tantrum at any moment. Evie wasn't sure she had the energy for one of her sister's fits right now.

Before Mia could protest, a shadow fell over them in the fading light. Evie looked up at the same time Mia let out a scream.

A man shrouded in black clothing stood holding a gun on them. Evie, too, let loose a shrill scream.

"Scream all you want. There's no one around to hear." The man gave a sharp laugh. "Besides, I'll have you tied up and loaded in the truck before anyone could get here anyway." He held up a wad of rope with his free hand and began to step toward her.

Evie glanced at Mia. Should she tell her to run? Was this man going shoot them? For some reason, she felt like it might be better for them to take their chances. She looked at the man inching toward them and then back at Mia before whispering, "Run!"

Mia sprinted off in the opposite direction of her sister. The man couldn't possibly chase them both, and to Evie's relief, he chose to follow her and not Mia. He didn't fire the gun, but ran after her instead.

Evie ran as hard as she could, but he eventually caught up to her. He dropped his gun as he latched his free arm around her and wrestled a hand over her mouth. Evie struggled to free herself before he could recover it and aim at her head.

The man wasn't overly large, but he was stronger than her. She ran out of energy quickly. When she had no fight left, she bit down hard on his finger. He released her, and she screamed as long and loud as she possibly could. If anyone was anywhere near them, she would make sure they heard her.

While her attacker was trying to shake off the pain from the bleeding wound on his finger. Evie socked him under the chin and rolled him while he wasn't expecting it. It didn't quite throw him off her, however, and he recovered quickly. He clapped a hand back on her mouth and punched her across the cheek with the other.

Evie managed to shrink away from much of the blow, but she was still a little stunned. Suddenly, a hand reached over from seemingly nowhere and pulled the brute off her.

Evie sucked in a breath, struggling to sit

upright and make sense of what was happening. Her rescuer made quick work of her attacker, laying him out with just a couple of fierce blows. She took him in with wide eyes and said a prayer of thanks.

Broad shoulders and a strong jaw were the first things she noticed about him. Definitely too handsome. He had lost his cowboy hat in the scuffle, and his wavy brown hair stood on end atop his head. Somehow it just made him more attractive.

Her rescuer discovered a wad of heavy twine in her assailant's pockets. He carefully secured some of it around the man's wrists and then did the same with his ankles. He finally looked at Evie once the man was lying unconscious at his feet. Piercing blue eyes nearly leveled her.

"Are you okay, ma'am?"

The deep voice was the last straw.

She crumpled back into a heap, eyes falling closed. "I'm fine."

"You don't look fine."

Was that laughter in his rumbly voice? She cracked one eye open to look at him. Yep. He was fighting a grin all right. She sat back up, one hand instinctively covering her throbbing cheekbone.

"Are you laughing at me? I just got attacked." She injected every ounce of indignation she had ever possessed into her words.

"You seem to have held your own." His amusement faded. "Any idea what this guy's doing out here? And better yet, what are you doing out here?"

She wrapped her arms around her waist protectively, and then she shot up, realizing she needed to find Mia. "My sister!"

Evie heard the man protesting as she dashed off after Mia, but she didn't slow. He caught up to her quickly and grasped her arm.

"I just wanna help. What's going on?" His brows were slightly furrowed and his steely jaw firm.

He was a little intimidating.

She stilled. "My name is Evie Langston. My sister, Mia, and I just moved to the area. I was camping with her when this guy showed up out of nowhere holding a gun on us. I told her to run hoping he would come after me, and he did. She ran off in the other direction. But now I've lost her."

Her rescuer glanced back at the man who had held the gun on them, still unconscious. He seemed to have come to a decision.

He nodded. "Let's go find your sister. He's not going anywhere."

Evie led him off in the opposite direction.

The terrain was a little unstable. Loose rocks and occasional rises in the landscape made her a little more careful of each step. They were in the beginnings of the foothills. She searched her surroundings as she went, yelling her sister's name.

When they made it back around to where Evie had begun to set up camp, she stopped for a moment. "I thought she'd have returned here. It's a pretty good distance to our ranch. At least a mile. Do you suppose she went all the way back to the house?"

He thought for a moment. "Maybe so. Let me see if I can get cell phone service. I need to call someone about that fella tied up in the pasture."

She nodded. He began to walk around, looking at his phone, and she finished packing up the camp hurriedly. She was anxious to find Mia, but she knew he was right. Her sister's safety depended on them taking care of the man who had attacked them.

"This is Beau Thorpe," she heard him say into the phone. Funny how she had trusted this man and hadn't even known his name.

Her wandering thoughts were rudely interrupted, however, as gunshots began to rain down on them from another direction. She suddenly realized her first attacker hadn't been alone.

Her rescuer dropped the phone and rushed at her.

"Get down!"

She did as he commanded, but a bullet grazed her left shoulder, and she fell off balance. She stumbled, but couldn't catch herself as she fell, her head connecting with a rock.

Everything went black.

Beau felt helpless as Evie fell to the ground. He was there just a second too late, and he lifted her into his arms after she collapsed.

There wasn't much out here in the way of shelter, but if he could make it across the field, there was a cave they could duck into until help arrived or they could shake off the shooter.

He looked at the petite, unconscious woman in his arms. Carrying her was easy, as she didn't weigh much.

He shielded her with his own body and deposited her in the shelter of a wide tree trunk. The shots seemed to be more to incite fear than cause harm, though. Many of the bullets struck so high up they hit sloping branches where they splayed out from the tops of the trees.

She began to stir, and it threw him off balance just as he was settling her against the trunk. He caught himself against the bark with a rough hand.

She began to struggle to get up. "Let me up. My sister!"

He gently pushed her back down. "You mentioned that. But you need to stay down."

"We can't leave Mia. We have to find her." The woman sounded frantic.

She finally settled momentarily in the shelter of the tree. "Can you wait here? I'll look. Be as still and quiet as you can until I get back. You won't be as easy to spot that way."

She nodded, and he lit out in search of the woman's sister. He didn't do much to try to avoid being seen, hoping he would draw attention away from where Evie was hidden.

He hadn't gone far past where he had first seen the woman when a girlish squeak came from almost underfoot. A thin frame hid trembling under some heavy underbrush.

"Mia?" He said the name to try to keep her from bolting.

Her wide eyes blinked as she tried to assess whether she should run or trust him.

"I'm here to help." He told the girl. She was smaller than he expected. "Your sister sent me."

"You almost stepped on me." She sounded more accusatory than frightened, and he had to admire her assertiveness. Standing, she brushed dirt and leaves from her clothes and hair.

"Sorry about that. We—"

"Is Evie okay?" The girl demanded to know about her sister despite the urgency of the situation.

"Evie's fine. But look, we have to move." A gunshot punctuated his words.

She shrieked and dived back into the bush.

"I've got you. Come on. Run in a zigzag. Follow me." Beau took off, and to his great relief she followed.

They crashed through the remaining trees and brush to where he had left Evie, and the younger girl ducked down beside her. "You left me."

Evie looked at her sister incredulously. "We had to do something. We were being attacked. I wasn't going to leave you."

"Where did you find this guy?" She gestured toward Beau. He wasn't sure how to react to her brash question. Amusement was his first instinct, but annoyance and insult were possibilities as well. She had quite a personality.

"He found me, actually. And you could consider that he is standing right there and be a little more polite." Evie said this softly, but her sister still looked annoyed by her correction.

Another shot brought them all back to the present issue.

And reminded him they needed shelter.

"We have to get out of these open woods before whoever's shooting gets close enough to hit someone." He picked Evie up and carried her once more. He didn't know how much damage she had done when her head struck the rock.

"I can walk," she protested. She sounded groggy. "I'm fine."

He grunted. "But can you run? We don't have time to waste."

He took off with her before she could argue further, making sure her little sister followed. Moving a little slower with her cradled in his arms, he ducked low and sprinted toward the cave. It was farther than he thought, however, and he was running out of steam by the time they got there.

Once inside, he laid her gently on the soft dirt in the tiny space, crouching beside her. Even in the dim light, he could see the crimson seeping through her shirt. He had to bandage her wound with something.

His hands were sticky from tending to her, but he managed to wipe them on his jeans well enough to work with them. His ranger survival skills came back to him in an instant, and he had her wound temporarily bandaged in seconds. It would need a proper cleaning as soon as they could get to some supplies, but for now it would stem the loss of blood.

Evie eyed him curiously despite her obvious pain as he was tying off the end of the makeshift bandage he had torn from the bottom of his long-sleeved shirt. The T-shirt he wore underneath was stained red from carrying her, and he hoped she hadn't lost too much.

"What now?" She started to rise.

"No, no, just stay put. I don't know how much damage you've suffered from the bleeding. And you hit your head." Beau put a hand on her stomach, but then realized what he was doing and jerked it away.

"It is beginning to hurt." Her right hand went to her temple. She looked confused. He hoped she didn't have a concussion as well. He told her little sister what had happened before he found her. Mia's eyes widened and she sucked in a breath.

There was one burning question that he had to ask, and Evie probably wasn't going to like it. But he didn't recognize her, and she'd said they just moved here. She was new in town, and he had a right to be suspicious considering all that had just happened.

"Tell me the truth. Are you in some kind of

trouble? I can't help you unless I know." He pinned her with a look he might have used on a subordinate in his days of military service.

She looked away. "No. I mean, I don't know. I'm not sure what's happening."

He waited in silence, and she finally continued. "My ex-boyfriend was involved in something shady that I never knew the details of. I just learned this morning he was found dead—a possible homicide. I don't know why anyone would be after me, though. We've been split up for months."

Should he believe her? Sure, she looked innocent enough, but he had been fooled by appearances before, especially where women were concerned. "How do you know he was involved in something if you don't know what it was?"

"It was his behavior. He became very secretive, and often angry. There were rumors that he had stolen money from a dangerous man, but of course, he wouldn't admit to it." She wrapped her arms around herself again. "Anytime I asked questions, he would tell me to mind my own business."

"But you didn't know anything about who he stole money from? You weren't involved?" Beau felt there had to be more to her story.

"Some man named Rich White. I didn't

know anything about it, really. I would have turned him in to the authorities if I had. No, all I knew was that Ruark quit his job, but somehow, he seemed to have more money than ever."

That was suspicious. But it didn't necessarily implicate her in any crimes. "I see. What was his excuse?"

"He said he cashed out his 401(k) because he had received a big business opportunity. But a friend of mine said she heard he'd gotten fired. He denied that, too, of course. That's when I ended things. I knew he wasn't being honest with me." She shivered. "Later I heard he'd stolen the money from a very powerful man. Apparently Rich White is the kind of man you shouldn't have dealings with."

Mia was acting disinterested in her corner of the cave, but Beau suspected she was taking in every word.

"I guess Ruark didn't take it well? When you ended things?"

"No, he..." She followed his gaze to Mia, and then she looked back up at him and froze as if just realizing what was happening. "Why am I telling you all this? I don't even know you."

"Because I'm trying to help you, but I have to know why." He relented when he considered it from her point of view, however. "Okay, you're right. You don't really know anything about me. My name is Beau Thorpe. My ranch is just across that fence there."

He paused to point out of the cave, but it was growing darker as they spoke, too dark to see his ranch well. "The Thorpe ranch has been in my family for generations. Ask anyone in town about me. I don't mind."

She gave a slow nod and he continued.

"I assume you're the new owner of the old Cohen ranch? I heard it was sold."

It was dark in the cave, but he could sense her change in demeanor. Her eyes glowed just a little despite the dim light, and he thought her shoulders slipped back a notch. "Yes, and I have plans to renovate and open a facility for equine therapy to treat PTSD and other psychological trauma. Horses are very therapeutic."

His stomach clenched. Post-traumatic stress disorder wasn't something he wanted to talk about. It was too close to home. He not only knew too many fellow rangers who had it, but he had suffered from PTSD himself.

Beau dismissed his thoughts. He would get her home safely and turn her protection over to the proper authorities. After that, he would probably rarely see her. He preferred to stay on his own ranch and keep to himself. He was managing his disorder just fine that way.

"And your sister is here visiting you?" He wasn't sure if he was redirecting his attention or hers. Not only had the young girl stopped listening, but she seemed to be asleep. Amazing.

"No, she lives with me. Our mother died not long after she was born." Her eyes grew slightly misty, if he wasn't mistaken.

"What about your father?" He hated to ask these personal questions, but he had to know. The answers might hold clues to why someone was after her.

"*My* father? My father disappeared when I was twelve. He was hiking in the mountains as part of a search and rescue crew, and they were caught in a wildfire. They never found his body." She pierced him with a hard gaze then. "*Her* father took a long weekend trip to Bali with his girlfriend six months ago, but his plane went down. They were both killed on impact."

He swallowed. Maybe she could relate to his problems from trauma. "I'm really sorry. So you are half sisters, then."

"Yes. It's all in the past. But she's struggling. I'm trying my best, but tonight's episode won't help her any." She straightened. "My name is Evie Langston. My sister is Mia Terrano."

A jolt of recognition went through him. "Oh. I heard about that plane crash. Her father was Davidoff Terrano?"

Evie looked at her hands. "The very one. She'll be very wealthy when she grows into her trust fund. That just makes my job of raising her that much more difficult."

He made a sound of agreement, then he leaned out of the cave to look around. "I think it's dark enough to head back. Our shooter seems to have given up for the night. My ATV is parked not far from here where I was checking some heifers and working on the fence. I'll go get it. It'll get us back to your place faster."

Evie looked down at her messy clothes and dusted off, wavering for a moment as she looked back up due to her injuries. He had almost forgotten them in the past few moments. She spoke, redirecting his thoughts. "Should we call the police?"

Beau nodded. "I already called the sheriff. He'll be on the property any moment now. But I doubt he'll find much until the sun comes up tomorrow. I don't have a good signal in this cave. I don't think we can get anything else to go through. We'll give it a little more time, and then I'll check things out."

Evie settled back into her spot against the cool rock wall of the cave. She closed her eyes for a moment. Her lovely face took on a relaxed, cherubic softness. She had a look of purity and innocence that pulled him in. He hadn't felt so drawn to anyone in a long time.

No more women in your life, Thorpe. You're happier single, he reminded himself. He had been burned too many times. Romance never seemed to work out for him, whether it was his fault or someone else's choice. But even if he tried again, soon enough she would be wishing for a man who didn't have all the baggage he had, at the very least.

For some reason, he and all his brothers had grown up with a bit of a hero complex. They had all chosen military or law-enforcement careers. And they all had the traumatic stories that went along with it. His brothers seemed to be overcoming theirs.

But Beau didn't know if he ever could.

Almost an hour later, he still had no signal, but all was silent outside. "Evie, I'm going to look around outside. If it's all clear, we will go for the ATV."

At her nod of agreement, he eased out of the cave. Nothing stirred. He walked all the way around, looking for any sign of life. When nothing and no one emerged, he went back for the girls.

Evie gently nudged Mia awake, and they followed Beau to the ATV. They piled on with Mia sandwiched between the two adults. He drove slow considering it was a two-person ATV.

He was surprised at how run-down the old Cohen place looked when he eased the vehicle to a stop in the yard. Truthfully, he didn't get off his ranch a whole lot, and he hadn't been this way in a while. It almost looked unlivable, and he cut his eyes to the little lady crawling out from behind him on the ATV. What was she thinking?

"You're living here?" The question was out before he could think better of asking it.

Mia snorted. He wasn't sure what that meant, but he thought she was less than pleased with the living arrangements as well. He could just imagine, if she was the child of wealthy Davidoff Terrano, the Italian millionaire.

A scruffy little dog came running at their approach, and Mia jumped off and ran toward it. "Harvey, I told her we should have taken you with us."

Evie, who still hadn't answered, was clearly ruffled by his incredulous question. "I know it needs some work. But it's…clean. And we'll get there."

"I'm sure it is. But…what if it rains? Have you checked the roof? And the windows?"

He ignored her huff as he moved in closer to examine the structure. Though the house was brick, he could see it had been neglected for decades. If the interior was anything like the overgrown yard and cracked windows, Evie was going to have some work ahead of her.

She followed him to the closest window. "It's sound enough."

But her voice didn't sound so sure. He cut her a look that said he noticed. "I can caulk these windows for you until you can get them replaced. But it's a temporary fix. The nights get very cold around here."

Her expression said it might be less temporary than he had in mind. "That would be nice. But I can't pay you much."

"I'm not asking for pay. Just being neighborly. I have the caulking on hand, and it won't take long." He grunted to emphasize his point.

"I don't want to accept charity." She crossed her arms. Did she think he saw her as someone to be pitied?

He thought for a moment. "Maybe we can come up with a fair trade."

She eyed him with a wary expression. She seemed unable to accept help, for some reason. "Like what?"

He chuckled. "I'm a terrible cook. We used to have a live-in cook, but she retired. If you can cook, I'll trade out some home improvement work for some home-cooked meals for me and my ranch hands. We've been taking turns cooking, but we've all lost a few pounds since Mrs. Donnelly left us."

She shrugged. "I'm a decent cook." Her attention was on the house, though. "Mia? Mia, where did you go?"

Her sister didn't answer, so she went to the door. He noticed the porch sagged dangerously beneath her feet. He shook his head.

He stepped carefully on the rickety porch boards as he followed her. It was clean. But it was nearly empty. No Mia.

"She's not in here," he told her as he stepped out.

"Where did she go? She was just here."

Beau looked around. "Is there anywhere else she might be?"

Evie was shaking her head, but at that moment he heard a noise coming from the barn.

"Do you hear that?" he asked.

She paused before bobbing her head in agreement. "It sounds like crying."

Evie sprinted to the barn, throwing the door open and running down the aisle. He trailed her, the crying growing louder.

She peeked into one stall, and then the next, until finally she stopped.

"Oh, Mia."

He peered over her shoulder and saw the tiny slip of a girl, curled into a ball and sobbing in the bottom of a dirty horse stall, the scruffy dog curled up beside her.

TWO

"Mia, please don't disappear like that." Evie folded her arms around her little sister, oblivious to the dirt and pine shavings that clung to her from the stall floor. Harvey, the little mutt they had adopted at the shelter, sniffed her, and moved over to let her closer. Mia just kept sobbing, her tiny form shaking with every gasp.

Evie just held her, rubbing her head, and let her get her cry out. When Mia's wails finally subsided to hiccups, she looked up.

"I thought—I was gonna lose you—too." Mia touched the bandage on her sister's shoulder, but when Evie shook her head in dismay at her sister's state, Mia buried her head in Evie's chest and sobbed once more.

"Oh, honey." Evie looked helplessly up at her rescuer.

Beau's eyes were full of sympathy, mixed with a little uncertainty. He was clearly uncomfortable in this situation.

Evie didn't really know what to do herself. It seemed the events of the day had finally caught up with her sister. Compassion for Mia flooded her, but words seemed out of reach. Everything that came to mind just seemed so trite. The hurt she felt for the little girl far outweighed the sting from her injury.

Finally, Mia's sobbing slowed, and she looked up at her sister with red-rimmed eyes. "This is all my fault."

Evie leaned back to look at her. "What on earth do you mean, Mia? How could it be your fault?"

The girl sighed. "Daddy told me there'd be bad men who were after me because of my money."

Evie looked at Beau, who was struggling to suppress a grin, unless she missed her guess. "Um, Mia, honey, I think he meant when you're older. You don't have access to any of the money yet. I suspect he meant when you're ready to marry."

"Ew!" Mia spat. "I don't ever wanna get married."

Evie allowed the grin to spread across her face then. "You might change your mind when you're older. Besides, he followed me, not you, when we ran. And I'm as poor as the proverbial church mouse. This isn't your fault at all."

Mia let out a breath. “Good. So why was he after you?”

Evie had been asking herself the same question. She was afraid of the answer. “I’m not sure.”

Tires crunching on the gravel outside the barn drew their attention.

“Who’s here?” It was Evie who asked the question aloud.

Beau ducked out of the barn to look. “It’s the sheriff. He’ll wanna talk to you both.”

Evie cringed. “Great.”

Beau gave her a strange look, head tilted slightly sideways. “Dean Sharum’s a nice guy. Nothing to worry about.”

Evie nodded but didn’t say anything else. She had certainly encountered more than one law-enforcement officer who wasn’t.

Beau was right, though. The sheriff shook her hand and quickly put her at ease. “It’s nice to meet you, Miss Langston, though I’m sorry it’s under these circumstances.” He glanced sympathetically at her bandaged shoulder. “We took the man into custody. A deputy trailed one of the men back to a clearing near the road on the south side of the ranch. It looked like they had a vehicle parked there, but he was gone before we could get there. What can you tell us about the attack?”

Evie explained what had happened, while a wide-eyed Mia nodded her agreement each time anyone looked her way. Beau listened silently, but Evie thought his expression got harder with every word. When she explained that the gunshot had happened after Beau had tied up the man they had in custody, the sheriff's eyes widened.

"All we really know is there were at least two men involved. We'll question the one in custody, but we likely won't be able to hold him long. He's already in the system and knows how this works. He'll post bail and be gone." He looked at Beau, who lowered his chin with a grim expression.

Evie answered the rest of his questions the best she could and apologized that she couldn't offer more in the way of help.

"Thank you, Miss Langston. We'll keep you informed of what we find out. I'll send patrols by here as frequently as we can spare to keep an eye on things as well." The sheriff shook her hand and spoke briefly to Beau before departing. He turned to give a brief wave in Mia's direction.

"I'll drive you to the hospital. You should probably have that shoulder looked at. And your head took a solid blow also." Beau's manner didn't make it appear to be a question.

Evie tried not to wince. She didn't have the extra funds to spend on hospital bills right now. "I'd rather not. The bleeding has stopped, and I really don't think the head injury is serious."

He eyed her suspiciously. No doubt he was wondering why she didn't want to see a doctor. "I'd feel much better if you got treatment."

She shook her head. "Mia can call emergency services if the need arises."

He didn't look happy about her decision, but he let it go. He walked her toward the house.

The dark night outside the barn suddenly seemed eerie and ominous. Beau was looking around. She wondered what he saw when he looked at her new home. Was he thinking she wasted her money? That she was overzealous for thinking she could make something of this ramshackle mess?

She didn't have to wonder for long.

"I'm not sure you two are safe here alone. They may have one man in custody, but with someone else involved, there's a chance they'll try again. Especially since they didn't finish what they started. I wish Dean would have posted a deputy here for the night. I know they probably don't have the manpower, but it would have made me feel much better about your safety." Beau started walking around then, as if assessing the safety of the property.

"We'll be fine. I have a pistol, and all the door locks are sound." Evie started walking along behind him, trying to see what he was seeing.

He stopped and faced her. "I'll give you my number, just in case. I can get here before anyone else since I'm just up the road. Don't trust anyone." He was peering intently at her, and the moonlight glinted in his eyes.

When he left, Evie took Mia into the house and began to help her settle down for a good night's sleep. It wouldn't be an easy feat considering all that had just happened.

After some warm Sleepytime tea and a story, Mia fell asleep. Evie felt the weight of exhaustion on her whole frame as she settled into her room for the night. She found her mind wouldn't slow down enough to let her sleep. She replayed everything that happened, wondering a million times why she had been targeted. Was she just some unlucky victim? No, the second criminal, the one who had shot at them, had disproved that theory. He was clearly backup of some sort. She just didn't know why.

But her gut told her it had something to do with Ruark.

A noise from down the hall startled her from

her thoughts. It had been a sort of clicking sound. Was someone trying to break in?

She was on her feet and across the hall to Mia's room in a flash, barely remembering to snatch up her cell phone on the way. A creak sounded from the living room—maybe the front door—just as she closed the door to Mia's bedroom. Her heart pounded so loudly she could hear the whooshing sound in her ears.

Mia sat up, rubbing her eyes as Evie heaved at the heavy dresser with all her might, trying to shove it in front of the door. "What's wrong? What are you doing that for?"

Evie held a finger to her lips, urging her sister to be quiet. Then she whispered, "I think someone's breaking in."

Mia's eyes widened, but she didn't scream, thankfully. She did, however, scramble from the bed and run over to help. Evie gave her a nod of thanks but didn't pause.

The dresser was barely lodged in front of the door when she heard footsteps against the hardwood floors of the hallway. She leaned against it before she pulled up Beau's number and sent him a text, her hands shaking so violently she could barely spell the words correctly. Before she could dial 911, however, someone rattled the doorknob and started shoving at the door. The dresser shook and this time Mia did scream.

"Get into the closet," Evie instructed her, whispering.

The thumping against the door continued, shaking the dresser as some brute pushed on it. Evie leaned against it with all her strength.

"Where's the money, lady? Tell us where Ruark left the money, and we'll leave you alone." The deep voice roared angrily through the door. "Hand over the cash or we will make your little sister pay, just like your boyfriend."

Evie shivered as the words washed over her in a jumble. Her suspicions were correct. How could she defend herself and Mia against grown men? And Ruark…oh, no. They thought she had the money Ruark was rumored to have taken.

So it was true?

Ruark had stolen money from a mob boss, and now they wanted it back.

They weren't going to believe she didn't have it.

Beau woke to the sound of his cell phone chiming. He had been dreaming about going down in a plane again, and he was sweating and shaking. The phone's ringtone helped to clear his head, however, making it easier to dispel the memories. He was slowly learning to shut them out, but the dreams clung to him.

Raising up to look at the phone, he realized Evie had texted him. Twice.

She was in trouble.

He jumped up and stumbled quickly into his clothes. How had he been so sound asleep that he hadn't heard it?

He tried not to think about what it could be and refused to let himself panic. It could be a false alarm. But his conscience told him he shouldn't have left them alone tonight. If he was a little more than normally concerned about the well-being of a neighbor he had just met, well, he wouldn't think about that either.

He got to Evie's place in just a few minutes, but everything was dark. He cut the engine to his truck and dashed to the house. His Glock was at the ready, even before he saw the front door swinging on its hinges.

As silently as he could, Beau followed the sound of someone banging against the door of a bedroom. When he rounded the corner to the hallway, he saw the black-clad figure heaving at the door.

"Hold it right there." His voice was commanding and full of authority.

The man did at first, then he did something stupid.

He tried to run.

But the only way out was down the hall and past Beau. As he tried to shove past, Beau aimed the Glock at the intruder's left leg and fired. It grazed one thigh. Blood soaked his jeans.

The black-clad man went down, screeching like a banshee. But when Beau tried to tackle him, the man managed to struggle to his feet. He landed a good hard blow to Beau's left cheek and took off. He limped down the hallway, knocking over furniture and a lamp on his way out. The obstacles were enough to slow Beau down just a little, but he was still close on the guy's heels.

Beau chased the limping man out of the house. He almost caught him at the end of the porch, but the man threw a rocking chair at him, sending him off balance long enough to get some distance between them again before tumbling off and rolling away. Before Beau could catch up again, he limped down the yard and hopped onto a motorcycle he had left at the edge of the road and took off.

Beau fired at the taillight a couple of times, but to no avail. The man was gone.

He made his way back into the house, dreading the task of telling Evie the man had gotten away. He wouldn't even consider the thought that she might be injured.

Nor would he consider why he didn't want to think about it.

"Evie, it's me. You can open the door. He's gone." Beau stood outside the door and waited.

When the scraping on the other side stopped and the door opened, a pale, terrified pair stood in the frame. He wanted to wrap his arms around them both.

"Are you both okay?" He looked them up and down.

"Y-yes, I think so." Evie was trying to be strong for her sister, but he could see she was shaking.

"Gather up what you both need for the night. I'm taking you to my place." Beau gestured in the general direction of his neighboring ranch.

Evie stood still for so long, he thought she was going to protest. Instead, she nearly broke his heart with her words.

"Really? You've already gone to so much trouble. And you don't even know us. You're that willing to trust two strangers and open your home?" She looked so taken aback, he almost didn't know what to say.

"I'm not the kind of guy to just leave a couple of ladies unprotected, just because I don't know them well." He shot her a grin. "Besides.

We're neighbors. We take care of our neighbors out here."

He thought her chin wobbled a bit before she smiled and looked away. She turned and began to help Mia gather her things.

"We'll take Harvey, too." Beau motioned toward the little dog, who had come running from the barn in time to chase the motorcycle away, barking.

Evie looked grateful for this little gesture as well. He knew Mia wouldn't want to leave her pup.

Evie's sister had been extremely quiet, and he noticed now that Mia was watching him curiously. What had happened to these two to make them so wary, so surprised to find kindness in others?

Beau called dispatch and updated the authorities on the emergency call while Evie and Mia packed what they needed. The police promised to be on the lookout for anything suspicious that might lead them to the perp, but he didn't expect anything to come of it. He would call the sheriff directly first thing tomorrow and talk to Dean. For now, the intruder was gone and there wasn't much that could be done.

Once they were at the Thorpe ranch, Mia perked up a bit. "This place is kinda cool."

Beau gave her a crooked grin. "Well, it's been in my family for four generations. So it's kinda old."

"Well, there's gross-old and there's cool-old. This place definitely isn't gross." Mia walked along the porch, taking in the wood beams and rough-hewn logs that made up the exterior of the house.

"It is beautiful," Evie agreed.

Beau eyed the log home with fresh eyes. "Yes, I've always thought so. I never thought I'd be the one to own it."

"What do you mean?" Evie furrowed her brow as she looked at him.

"I have four brothers. And I'm a twin. It seemed unlikely that I'd be the one to end up with it. My brothers all went in other directions, though, and I ended up buying them all out. I'm the only one that came back and wanted to stay." Beau opened the front door.

Both females let out a gasp. The hand-carved stairway right off the entry and the massive river stone chimney did make for quite the first impression. The chimney was edged with beautifully stained logs and accented with a rough-hewn log mantel that stretched a good ten feet across. The windows on either side stretched up high, and the hardwood, knotted pine board floors completed the scene. Cozy rugs, one cowhide before the fireplace, and others accented the rest of the floor.

"I saw something like this at a resort one time in Colorado." Mia's voice held considerable awe. "And you *live* here?"

Beau nodded, humbled by the admiration.

He showed the ladies to a couple of spare bedrooms typically occupied by his brothers when they came to visit, though Evie protested that they could share a room. He saw no reason for them to have to share a space, and since Mia seemed enthralled with the place, Evie finally consented to sleep in separate rooms.

It didn't take long for Mia to fall asleep again once she was settled. Harvey had curled up on the rug beside her bed. The ease with which she was able to go back to sleep surprised Evie as much as it did Beau.

"Kids really are resilient. I don't know how she's already fast asleep again with all this going on." Evie looked pretty worn out herself but was clearly too shaken to sleep.

"I guess so. Or she's just exhausted. I'm glad she feels comfortable enough here to relax, though." Beau glanced at the empty fireplace silently praying the ladies would be as safe here as he hoped.

"That man said something tonight." Evie looked nervous about bringing it up.

He nodded to encourage her.

"He asked where Ruark's money was. I think they believe Ruark told me where he put the money or that I have it. I'd hoped it wasn't true and that there was another explanation. But it seems it might be true after all." Evie swallowed. "How could I have been so blind as to trust him?"

He waited a moment, but she didn't look at him. "You believe this proves your suspicions to be true? That he took a large sum of money from someone dangerous?"

"It would seem so. I'm starting to think maybe whoever it was killed him for it. What I don't know is why he got mixed up in this situation to begin with, or why these men think I have the money." She still wasn't looking at him.

He wanted to believe it was just from embarrassment. But it could also be from guilt. His instincts told him she was telling the truth, but he didn't know how to be sure. After all, he had just met her. He knew nothing real about her.

She looked at him then with fear in her eyes. "There's no telling what he could have told them about me. I just know Ruark Beaty wasn't a good person." Her eyes were pleading. And the most unusual violet-blue color, he couldn't help noticing.

"Look, I want to help you. But I need to know everything to protect you. Everything." His voice came out gruff.

She winced in response. "I'm doing my best. I just can't think of anything important that I haven't told you."

"Well, maybe you need to sleep on it. For now, how about we clean up that wound a little better and rebandage it. I'd feel better if you didn't go to sleep right away after hitting your head." He rose to get first aid supplies.

"Thank you." She nodded.

He remained silent as he cleaned and dressed her shoulder. It was hard not to wince each time she sucked in her breath at the sting, but he didn't have the numbing agents available at the hospital. He was glad to see it didn't need stitches.

When they had finished up and she let out a sigh of relief, he reiterated what he had told her before. "I know you're overwhelmed right now, but I'll be awake. If you think of anything, let me know. If anything else happens, just yell and I'll be right there."

He waited for her to give her assent, then he watched her rise and make her way up the stairs to the room he had shown her earlier. It was right across the hall from his own.

Which was part of the reason he couldn't sleep.

True, he had wanted her close. But he hadn't felt this much protectiveness—and tenderness—toward any woman in a long time.

He had hoped he never would again.

Worse, there was something about Evie that reminded him of Caitlyn. And if there was anyone he didn't want to be reminded of, it was her. He had spent the past four years trying to forget.

He focused his thoughts instead on Evie's predicament. Was she truly innocent in all this? Could she be hiding something after all? Or was he simply letting his fears make him suspicious where there wasn't cause?

It was after 3:00 a.m. before Beau was finally able to sleep. Though he was normally an early riser, the sun was creeping up the walls of his room when he awoke the next morning. He rose, showered, and dressed quickly to go check on his guests.

The door to Evie's room stood open and the bed was neatly made. Maybe she was downstairs or with Mia.

But Mia's door stood open as well.

He made his way down to the kitchen, checking the living room on his way. They weren't anywhere in the house. Surely she hadn't been foolish enough to take off back to her house alone. But calling their names got no answer. After a few minutes of calling and searching, one thing was certain.

They were nowhere in the house.

THREE

Evie had almost forgotten about the danger of the night before just listening to her sister laugh and chatter about the horses. Mia was smiling again for the first time in weeks. It made her feel more confident in her decision to move to Wyoming and her plan to begin the therapeutic riding center. Just the soothing act of stroking the muzzle of a big bay gelding gave her a sense of peace she hadn't felt in a long time, especially in the past twelve hours. She couldn't wait to find the horses for her own ranch. She had been in contact with a few sellers, but so far hadn't had a lot of success.

When Beau came storming into the barn, however, everything changed.

"What do you think you're doing?" His voice boomed from the door of the barn, making Evie shrink from him. It brought back memories of the angry moments after Ruark had begun to change.

"We wanted to see the horses." Mia chirped the response as if she hadn't even noticed his angry tone.

Evie swallowed back her thoughts and tried for the same bravado. "You weren't up and about yet. She asked if we could come to the barn. I really didn't think you'd mind."

"I have no problem with you coming to the barn. It's the going off alone and not telling anyone that I have a problem with." He didn't sound quite so gruff this time, but the reprimand still stung.

"Right. Well, now that you're about, we'd like to go home." Evie looked away, blinking back the moisture threatening to spill over in her eyes.

That set him back on his heels just a bit. "I'm not sure that's a good idea."

"You can't babysit us forever." Evie braced her fists on her hips. She had to rely on herself. It was too dangerous to depend on a man. They could change in an instant.

"You think it's safe for you to go off on your own right now? You were almost kidnapped yesterday. Someone broke into your house. Your sister is in the middle of all this danger. I think it's in both of your best interests to have a babysitter right now." His whole demeanor spoke of determination.

She really couldn't argue with that. She considered him. "Well. I guess you're right. What can I do to compensate you? I don't want to feel like I'm putting you out."

"Like I said, I need someone to cook. But I have a half-dozen hands coming and going, aside from the four that live on the ranch." Beau looked around. "That might be a bigger job than you're up for."

Mia was still chattering pleasantly at one of the horses, but Evie just looked at her and nodded. "I can handle cooking for a crowd. I worked in food service as a work study job while I was in college."

"Good. How about we go pick up whatever things you and Mia need to stay here for a few days. We can hash out the details later." Beau gestured toward the door of the barn.

Evie spoke to Mia softly. "Are you okay with that?"

Her little sister sent her a look that said it was a silly question to ask. "Duh."

Evie just shook her head at her.

"Let's get that done, then." Beau led them from the barn to his black truck, waiting in the drive.

It was a short ride, and when they pulled into the drive of Evie's much smaller place, she saw it through his eyes. The small ranch house looked neglected and old. Its windows were taped over where they had been cracked. The wooden eaves and trim, never replaced with vinyl siding, looked weathered and rotten. The barns, too, were in much need of repair, the wood cracked and speckled with peeling paint. Sagging doors strained the hinges and wide crevices let the wind blow right through. One smaller outbuilding looked as if a little wind might send it sprawling.

"The place does need a lot of repairs. I can see it finished as a beautiful haven for therapy, but it's going to take a little while." She spoke in a low voice. Did he think she had taken on too much with this huge project? The porch sagged, and big bare patches speckled the roof where shingles had gone missing, but when Evie had purchased it she'd seen only the potential. Starting a center for equine therapy had been her dream for at least a decade, and she wouldn't give up on it now.

"I admire your vision. I've wanted to see this place brought back to life for some time. But I'm afraid my best idea would have been to demolish it and start over. It takes courage to take on a job like this. I'm glad for people who have that courage." Beau pulled to a stop in the driveway. When he looked at Evie, sincerity emanated from his eyes.

"I hope I can pull it together." Evie hated to admit it, but the task was daunting. "I've applied for a grant to help me pay for repairs and supplies, and I hope to get started very soon. I'm not sure how long it will take to hear back about the grant, but I plan to use what resources I have in the meantime...at least until they run out. I have a background in agriculture and a minor in psychology, and I believe it will be beneficial to so many to have a therapeutic place in this area."

She felt like she might be saying too much—babbling, even—but the look Beau wore said he understood.

Evie stepped out of the truck and turned to help Mia, but she had just pulled open the door when a terrifying *ping* sounded way too close to her left shoulder.

A shout echoed through the air. "Give yourself up, lady, and no one else will get hurt."

She dropped to the ground, even as Beau was commanding her to do so. He was barking out orders for Mia as well, instructing her to get onto the floorboard of the truck. As he did so, more bullets flew. Evie had a hard time keeping her head down. She wanted to look for the shooter, but no one was visible from her vantage point. All she could see was Beau pulling his own weapon from a holster at his waist as he ducked around the front of the truck to her side.

"Call for help." He took his phone out of his back pocket with his free hand. "Call 911 first. Once they disconnect, call Dean. The sheriff's number is in emergency contacts."

She did as he instructed, and while the 911 dispatcher promised someone was on the way, Sheriff Dean Sharum pronounced he was headed there himself. Bullets kept coming sporadically. All they could do was use the truck for cover, Beau occasionally firing back.

"I can't get a read on his exact location. I feel like I'm just wasting ammo at this point. How long?" Beau glanced at her quickly just before another bullet whizzed by far too close for comfort.

"Five minutes." Evie didn't say it, but that seemed like an eternity in a situation like this.

"Ugh. I guess I'm going to have to waste more ammo then." Beau leaned around the open door and fired back in the shooter's direction.

"Can you see anything?" Evie couldn't keep quiet. Nervous chatter, her grandpa had always called it.

"Nothing. Not even a flash of light off his weapon. But he's somewhere in those trees.

That's the only place he could find that much cover." He aimed the pistol again.

She leaned close. "There's an old well just inside the tree line. The shadows would be covering it right now because of the angle of the sun. I'd guess that would be his hiding place."

Beau glanced over his shoulder at Evie, and her breath caught at the intensity of his blue eyes in the morning light. "Where?"

It took her a second to recover and respond. *Stop it!* she told herself. "Just to the right of that big oak tree in the center. I'd say no more than ten yards to the right."

He nodded, took aim, fired, and was rewarded with the sound of exploding rock and a yelp. "Good thought. I like it."

She felt laughter welling up. It was totally inappropriate, but something in his tone got to her. "I'm glad."

He reached back and squeezed her hand unexpectedly, and she felt a jolt. All thoughts of laughter fled. He must have felt the same, for he turned and looked at her, eyes full of questions.

He didn't ask them, though. He couldn't have if he had wanted to, for just then the shooter recovered and fired again.

When the bullet glanced off the back passenger window, shattering the glass, Mia shrieked.

"Just hold tight, honey." Evie tried to reassure her. "Help is on the way."

"Okay." Mia mumbled the word from deep in the back seat, but her voice was shaking.

"How long?" Beau was aiming again. "Magazine is almost empty."

"Three more minutes. According to the dispatcher, anyway." Evie was looking at her watch. She jumped when his Glock fired again.

"At least he doesn't seem inclined to come any closer." Beau squinted toward the trees. "Check in the console of my truck. I might have some ammo stashed there in case of an emergency. Just stay low."

She ducked onto the floorboard of the truck, raising her hands to the latch on the console cover. As she lifted it, more glass shattered. This time it was the front window. It held its shape, but spiderwebs of cracks covered the entire passenger side of the windshield. Her scream came instinctively.

"Don't worry about the ammo. Another shot might dislodge the whole windshield. I don't want you in there if it does." Beau was looking at her over his shoulder again. "It shouldn't be much longer."

"Evie, I don't like this! Make it stop!" Mia pleaded.

"I know, sweetheart. I don't like it either.

Soon. The deputies will be here soon." Evie tried to sound convincing, but she wanted it to stop also. It was tearing her nerves to shreds.

Beau must have sensed her crumbling composure. His voice was soothing and gentle. "Just hold on. It's going to be okay."

Evie wanted to curl up on the floorboard of the truck like Mia, but she had a responsibility to be strong for her little sister. It was the last thing she wanted to do right now, though.

She squeezed her eyes shut for a moment, uttering a silent prayer. A faint whine came to her. Sirens? She strained to hear better. In a blink, they grew more defined, and she let out a breath of relief.

"They're coming." She said it loud enough for Mia to hear as well as Beau.

"Good. I think I have one bullet left in the magazine. If he runs, maybe I can wing him." Beau grunted.

A few more shots and then the shooting stopped as the patrol cars from the sheriff's office pulled into the driveway. The shooter never appeared. If he ran, it must have been out the other side.

The sheriff was the first one to reach them. "In the trees?"

When Evie and Beau both nodded, he pulled his service weapon. "I'm going after him."

The deputies jumped out of their vehicle and followed, but Beau stayed by Evie's side. In a few minutes, they came back toward them, empty-handed and with disappointment on their faces.

"He got away." Beau made the statement, but it only echoed Evie's thoughts.

"It looks that way. I think maybe we should sit down and talk about what's going on here." Dean looked from one to the other.

"My ex-boyfriend was rumored to have stolen money from a powerful man. These men seem to think I have access to what he stole. I don't know anything about it, though. I hadn't even spoken to Ruark in months," Evie explained.

Dean asked her a few more questions about the details and she answered him stiltedly, her adrenaline still in effect.

"I know you don't want to hear this, but these men aren't the kind to give up easily." Dean was writing something in a small notebook in his hand.

She could feel the shaking beginning in her center. "So he's going to try again."

Dean's nod was full of sympathy.

Beau pulled her close and tucked her against his shoulder. "It'll be okay. We'll get him. I won't let up until we do."

* * *

Beau wasn't sure where all these tender feelings were coming from, but he meant what he told Evie. The stark bruise across her delicate cheekbone stood out in contrast to her fair skin and made her look even more vulnerable today. He was going to find whoever was behind these attacks on her and see him brought to justice. There was no way this guy was going to get away with terrorizing her like this, and whether it was about the money her former boyfriend supposedly took or not, he would make sure she was safe. He wouldn't rest until he was sure she was.

The tenderness he was feeling for her, however, was a problem. He didn't want to fall in love. He had decided long ago to remain a bachelor, dedicating his life to keeping his father's legacy afloat. He had been the reason one of his fellow Rangers had died, leaving behind a wife. Canaan had been one of the finest men Beau had ever known. Beau didn't deserve that kind of happiness after what he had done. The loss haunted him every day.

He was determined not to focus on his past or on Evie and the gentle feelings she provoked as he waited for her to gather some belongings. She had been visibly shaken after the recent attack, but finally calmed enough to go inside.

She had waited patiently while he checked out every room in the house, and when he gave the okay, Mia had hurried to her room to get her suitcase.

Evie, however, hadn't been so eager to get her things. She had offered him a drink, talked about the house and made other mundane remarks until it was obvious she was trying to delay the inevitable.

She was nervous about staying at his place.

He could certainly understand that. After all, she barely knew him. She had no idea what to expect.

He pondered how he might put her at ease, but nothing came to mind. He finally decided to just try to make her comfortable. "I'm sorry about all this."

"It isn't your fault at all. And you've been nothing but kind. I appreciate your help. I might have been killed if not for you." She relaxed a bit. He hoped she knew he was on her side.

They gathered the bags to go. Beau was anxious to get back to his ranch. There was safety in numbers, and now that the sheriff and deputies had cleared out, he wasn't feeling quite as safe as he had before. The guy shooting at them earlier had managed to escape, so he could easily plan another attack right away.

"Let me check to see that it's all clear before you and Mia leave the house." He went to the truck and pulled his gun out of the console to reload when a thought struck him.

He approached the door. "Evie, did you say you have a gun?"

She nodded. "Yes, it's in my bedroom tucked under the mattress."

He returned the gesture. "You might wanna get it. Just in case. And any extra ammo you have. Keep it on you at all times."

She ducked back into the bedroom. He heard her shuffling some things around, and then she reappeared. "Done."

She showed him her gun and then stuck it in the waistband at the small of her back. She also handed him some nice binoculars. "These were my dad's. They might help."

"Okay. Let's be quick." Beau accepted the binoculars and opened the door.

He eased out, looked around, then raised the binoculars and scanned the trees. Nothing stirred. His instincts said they were all clear.

He motioned Evie and Mia forward. "It's clear. We'll have to take your truck, Evie. I can't drive mine until the windshield is repaired. Here we go. Stay low."

The two women did as he asked. Mia stayed silent through all this, and he was thankful. A terrified child would bring added stress to both him and Evie. He couldn't help thinking maybe Mia had seen some things in her young life.

Evie motioned for him to drive as they approached the truck. He climbed behind the wheel, adjusting the seat for his long legs.

Before starting the vehicle, he looked at them both, securely belted in. "Everyone good?"

They responded with an affirmative.

"Get us out of here." Mia crossed her arms, but her eyes searched their surroundings.

He backed from the driveway and pulled onto the road. Suddenly, he wasn't feeling as confident that they would make it back to his ranch safely. He sensed something wasn't right.

He hit the gas, thinking maybe they should hurry. His speed increased as much as he dared on the loose gravel of the small county road.

But when they rounded a slight curve, he realized speed would do them no good. He slammed on the brakes and sent the truck into a skid. Mia shrieked. Evie gasped.

The road was blocked by half a dozen men holding rifles.

FOUR

Evie felt her blood go cold—so cold she wasn't sure it was still flowing.

What could they possibly do against a small army holding automatic rifles? It seemed hopeless.

Beau slammed on the brakes and the truck slid sideways to a stop. He jerked the wheel hard and punched the gas before they had even stopped skidding, fishtailing off in the other direction.

"Get down!" Beau shouted the command to both females just before shots peppered the tailgate and back bumper. A pop sounded, and the truck spun out of control.

"One of the tires is hit." Beau made the grim pronouncement just before they settled against the steep side of the ditch along the dirt road. "They are trying to force us out so they can get to you. We'll have to run."

Nausea swelled in her stomach. How were

they going to get away on foot when these men had high-powered weapons? She had no doubt they wouldn't mind winging her to slow her down enough to catch her. She glanced at Mia and found her little sister pale and wide-eyed. Terror radiated from her, and she looked frozen to the seat. Would they hurt her sister to get her to cooperate?

Beau took action, jumping out and opening Mia's door. "Come to me, Mia. Get on my back. We have to go."

To Evie's surprise, Mia instantly complied, sliding across the seat and onto his strong back. Evie slid from the passenger seat and ducked low to follow them at a quick sprint. They ran for the cover of the stand of trees not far off the road. Cottonwoods jumbled with some juniper and fir trees to make an odd mishmash of cover, but it was thick, and she was thankful. Though it made it harder for them to trek through it, the trees also made them difficult to see or hit with the rifle fire.

Beau's stamina was impressive. Even with Mia on his back, he didn't slow, only looked back to be sure Evie was keeping up as they pressed through the heavy foliage. She could hear footsteps crashing into the trees in pursuit, and Beau urged her on.

Her pulse pounded, not only from fear but

also the exertion of stepping carefully over rocks and roots at such a rapid pace. She found herself wheezing as the air seemed less effective at providing her lungs with the required amounts of oxygen.

"Are you okay?" Beau whispered the words just loud enough for her to hear. How was he breathing so normally with Mia on his back?

She could only nod as he continued on.

Voices sounded behind them.

"We'll find them. There's nowhere for them to go," a cruel voice said.

"I hope you're right. We need this done quickly." Another voice didn't seem as easily convinced.

Beau's eyes met hers and he shook his head. What was he trying to tell her? He wouldn't speak for fear of giving them away, but Mia looked like she might begin to whimper anytime.

Evie watched him give Mia's calf a reassuring pat. Amazingly, her sister calmed, tightening her grip around Beau's shoulders. Evie had to temper her own reaction to his tender gesture as he motioned her on.

She pushed herself to her limits, realizing the steepening terrain was part of the reason for her fatigue. Her legs burned along with her lungs, and she closed her eyes to try to think of something besides wanting to stop.

Just when she thought they might be losing the gunmen, the edge of the trees began to lighten. They were coming to the end of the wooded area. What would they do now? Even if their pursuers were gaining on them, at least they were difficult to see in the darkened woods.

"Evie, we're going to have to make a break for it across the clearing. They'll see us as soon as we emerge, but if we can get across the clearing, there's an old work shed out there on the other side. We can barricade ourselves in there until help arrives. Do you think you have the energy for one last sprint?" Beau was looking at her hopefully.

She honestly didn't know if she had it in her or not. But she had to try. It was their only hope. She nodded, sucking in huge gulps of air, trying to recover as much as possible before having to push herself once again.

"Okay. Once we take off, don't stop moving, no matter what. Stay as low to the ground as you possibly can while you're running and go as hard as you can the whole way. Understand?" Beau wore the look of a commander.

"Yes. I understand." She gulped in more air.

"Okay. Here we go." He sprinted off and

she followed immediately. They hadn't made it more than a few yards before the rat-a-tat-tat of the rifles began to sound.

Evie screamed. There was no way they could all survive this kind of assault, was there? She ducked lower and pumped her legs harder still. Silently she prayed. She prayed for protection for Beau and Mia. And she prayed for the physical strength to make it through this.

She felt like she might die of suffocation before they made it to the shed. Panic filled her. She couldn't breathe. She really couldn't. Suddenly, she wasn't sure if she was going to pass out, throw up, or both.

The old shed appeared at last. They ran through the door as more shots peppered the wood slat sides of the structure.

Evie slammed the door shut and bolted it as Beau deposited Mia carefully onto the floor. He immediately began to move an old, discarded woodstove over to the doorway. Evie collapsed into herself, trying to pull enough air into her body to survive.

"Call 911. Get us some help here ASAP." Beau had his gun drawn, but it was practically useless against the AKs their pursuers were wielding. Evie still had her gun in the waistband of her pants as well and she pulled it and followed him, still struggling for enough air.

Evie did as Beau suggested but the call was patchy, and she couldn't get a lot of details through to the dispatcher. Hopefully it would at least bring someone looking for them. In any case, making the call didn't bring her any comfort. After her weak attempts to speak to the dispatcher, she looked at Mia before speaking to Beau again.

"I'm not sure she really understood what was going on. She kept saying she couldn't hear me well. What can we do? There's not much chance of holding them off." Evie shook her head hopelessly. "It's going to take help a while to arrive, if they find us at all."

"Stay low and hang tight. We won't waste bullets fighting unless they come closer. I just hope we aren't giving them what they want by letting them surround us." Beau scanned the dusty old shed. It was old and tired looking, but the structure was still sound.

"Why doesn't anybody use this anymore?" Mia followed his gaze. "It looks better than Evie's house."

Evie gasped. "Mia!"

Her sister simply shrugged. "Well, it's true."

"It's unkind to point it out." Beau seemed to be trying hard to hide a grin as he spoke the words to Mia in a stage whisper. Then he answered her question in a normal voice. "I don't use this one anymore because I don't need it. The ranch is big, and this was an easy access point to work on broken-down equipment without having to bring it all the way to the main house and barns. Our operation isn't as large as it used to be, though, and we can use UTVs to haul what we need to the equipment if necessary. This one was once part of the original homeplace."

Their pursuers had gone oddly quiet. "What's going on?" Evie whispered the words.

"I don't know, but don't go sticking your neck out to find out." Beau eased over to the window. He kept his broad frame back in the shadows as he tried to peek out.

A pounding on the door startled all of them. "Might as well come out. We'll be right here waiting whether you come now or later."

Evie couldn't restrain her shiver.

Beau put a finger to his lips just in case Mia was considering a reply. The little girl shook her head, indicating she wouldn't do that.

When nothing changed, a hail of bullets sprayed across the side of the shed once more. One of the men hooted like an outlaw in an old Western. Evie winced and held in the gasp she wanted desperately to emit. Mia also made a face, but she didn't make a sound. It made

Evie wonder just what her sister had endured already in her short life.

"It's hard to fight back with only two guns against all those men." Mia pondered this fact aloud after a few seconds passed.

"She's right. We don't have a lot to fight back with." Evie shook her head. "We're sitting ducks. How will anyone find us here to help?"

Beau pressed his lips together. "Probably won't. We're going to have to get out of this on our own. Somehow."

"Can we make weapons? Something bigger?" Mia asked. "There's a lot of junk left over in here."

Evie looked to the corner where Mia gestured. A pile of discarded tools, buckets and other equipment sat sadly rusting there. She didn't really see anything useful.

Beau disagreed, however. "That's a great idea, Mia."

He strode over to the pile and began digging through it. He pulled out some large, dirt-encrusted glass bottles that looked like they had been used to doctor cattle at one time. Then he started digging through the buckets and other containers.

"Watch for spiders." Evie was terrified of the critters.

Beau chuckled. "Of course."

"Evie hates spiders." Mia injected the comment as she came closer to help Beau. "What are we looking for?"

"I think," Beau began, setting out a bucket full of rusty nails and fencing supplies, "we might be able to make some crude explosives. Ever heard of a Molotov cocktail?"

Mia giggled. "I'm too young for cocktails."

"This is a different kind. This kind might run off our bandits." He winked at her. "It's a homemade firebomb. We put some diesel in, add a rag and light it. We can use it to distract these guys long enough to make a run for it. I might even be able to find a way to make it explode just a bit."

"Well, we have bottles, and we have diesel. We can get some fabric from our clothes. Where do we get the stuff that makes it explode?" Mia scrunched up her face.

Evie was looking on, watching the two interact with a pang. Beau was so patient with her, explaining everything without a hint of irritation. She wasn't sure if Mia had ever had that. And even worse, it created a longing in Evie as well.

But the urgency created by the occasional spray of bullets from their attackers served as a reminder they were there and pulled her attention away from her missed opportunities.

"I'm going to look around. There's a chance there might be some fuel containers stored somewhere. The hands like to keep a little spare out here when they are working so they don't have to go all the way back to the barn if they need it." Beau was explaining this to Mia.

The shed was large enough to accommodate a decent-sized tractor, so he walked to the other end and began to investigate storage shelves. The shelves, too, were dusty and coated with spiderwebs and filth.

"Can I help?" She made the offer as she rose and strode over to the shelves where Beau crouched to look.

"Yes, just stay low. Who knows when they might spray another round at the shed." He gestured to a splintered place just above her head.

Evie ducked down. "Right. What will the container look like?"

"Just a typical fuel container, like you might fill up for a mower at the gas station or something." Beau was squinting at the shelves, but it was a little dark in this corner.

Evie pulled out her phone and activated the flashlight. "There."

She shone the light on a red plastic container on a low shelf. Beau reached for it with a grin. "Why didn't I think of that?"

While they worked, Beau talked to Mia about being an Army Ranger. "I was almost a pilot, but I decided I like being a paratrooper better. I did learn to fly, though."

Mia chattered back at him, and Beau looked over at Evie with a crooked, heart-stopping grin.

Evie smiled back, her heart reacting unexpectedly. What was it about this man that had her feeling this way? Sure, he was handsome, kind and patient. But she knew better than to get romantically involved with another man.

He was oblivious to her reaction, however. Beau had turned to Mia and held up the gas can. "Want to help me make some cocktails?"

Mia grinned. "Of course!"

"The trick is going to be getting a little gunpowder out of some of my bullets." Beau was explaining this to Mia as well, but he glanced at Evie. "Can you help Mia make the bottles, and I'll work on the gunpowder?"

Evie and Mia went to work, filling the bottles with rusty old nails and other bits of leftover fencing materials. The old bent clips that went on the post snapped easily to slip into the bottles also. While they did this, Beau carefully separated a couple of bullets, using spent casings from the few shots he had fired. The ends would slip over the unused bullets, and he could then gently ease the new bullets apart. The job looked tedious, but he patiently kept at it, even amid the occasional round of gunfire and ridiculous hooting from the men keeping them hostage here.

When he had extracted the gunpowder, Beau found some rags to soak in the diesel to use for bottles also. He tucked a bit of the ends of them into the bottles and left the rest hanging out the top to light. Once the explosives were ready, he explained the plan.

"We'll take opposite sides of the shed and count down before we throw them. If we throw them at the same time, maybe it'll make a big enough ruckus to send them packing. We'll go in two rounds." Beau handed two of the explosives to Evie carefully.

"What about me? Don't I get to throw some?" Mia was looking gravely offended.

Beau looked at Evie. She wasn't sure it was a good idea for her sister to be involved. "I don't know, Mia."

"I helped make them. I should get to throw some, too, shouldn't I? It's just like those firecrackers we used to play with." Mia braced her fists against her hips as if she was ready for a fight.

"These make a little bigger boom than a

package of ladyfingers." Beau tilted his head at her.

"I'll be super careful. I promise. Please?" Mia sounded older than her years.

Evie and Beau exchanged another glance, and Evie finally nodded. "Okay. Don't make me regret agreeing to this, though."

She wanted to be the fun sister—not that this was fun exactly. More importantly, though, Mia needed a mother figure in her life. A parent figure of any kind, really. She wasn't sure she was making the right decision. Worry settled in the pit of her stomach. Mia had always been indulged. She knew that because it had made her hard to handle ever since she came to live with Evie. But this wasn't a battle Evie had time to fight right now. They needed to get out of here and call the authorities.

Mia was beaming with confidence. "Awesome. Which side do I get?"

Beau pointed her in a direction and gave her careful instructions. They cautiously opened the window shutters enough to make them easy to get out of. Evie watched their interactions with another pang. He seemed so naturally good with Mia. It made Evie both envious and happy. It was too bad, really. Her sister could use someone like Beau in her life, but

Evie couldn't make the mistake of letting another man in her life.

Mia was holding her bottle carefully, giving Evie an impatient look. "Well? Are you ready or not?"

Evie nodded, and Beau motioned for her to take up position. "I'll count down from three, and we'll all throw the first round at once. The shutters are unlatched, so you should be able to push it free at the last second and throw. While those are still exploding, we'll throw the second round."

Another round of fire hit, causing them all to shrink back from the windows.

"Stay low until I say go," Beau instructed.

He began to count down.

At the last second, the trio pushed their shutters open and tossed the explosives. Evie was satisfied to hear a great boom as they all went off at once. Half a second later, Beau nodded at them, and they threw the second round. A yelp told them one of their attackers had been hit by some flying debris. When she looked over, Beau had his Glock out and ready to fire. Evie pulled her 9 mm as well.

"Come on. They seem to be scattering. Mia, stay between us." Beau led the way to the door.

He eased it open and looked, then motioned for them to follow.

They ran for the main road, but their attackers recovered quickly. It wasn't long before more shots began to echo around them. They had to stay low as they ran through the thick brush covering the open pasture, even though they had gotten a good head start on their pursuers.

The road was just yards away, however, when a command from a deep voice made them halt where they were.

"Everybody stop right there!"

FIVE

Beau turned slowly, doing his best to shield Mia and Evie from whoever was there. His blood had gone cold and still, as he thought he had just put them all in grave danger.

"Is that you, Beau?" the voice asked.

Relief swept through him. "It's me. I'm so glad you found us."

Sheriff Dean Sharum motioned back toward the dirt road. "The patrol car called in and said they saw Evie's truck out on the edge of the highway with a busted tire. Figured there was more trouble. I was headed there when dispatch came through with your call. I decided I'd better get here first."

More shots were fired then, and Dean and Beau pushed Mia and Evie down into the ditch. Both men had their weapons drawn, and Dean pulled his radio from his vest.

He spoke into the device, requesting backup

and giving their approximate location. When he finished, he turned to Beau. “We should be able to hold them off until Daniels and Stephens get here. They’re not far.”

“There’re at least five of them, but one or two might be injured. We can gather up some of my hands to help us out as well. Our phones weren’t working well way out here, or I would have called sooner. We barely got the call through to dispatch.” Beau gestured to the shed they had just evacuated.

“I’ll radio for someone to stop by your barn.” Dean did as he promised, but then went back to helping Beau fire back at their pursuers.

The sound of sirens approaching sent relief coursing through Beau in the next instant. The shooters were getting far too close for his comfort with their automatic rifles and seemingly unending supply of ammo.

The shooting stopped, then, and he heard the men fleeing. A few had run back to their vehicles and brought them round closer to their current location and they made a run for them now.

The sheriff motioned for Beau and the ladies to stay put while he hurried over to direct the deputies. They went off in pursuit, but their attackers had already jumped into waiting vehicles and peeled away from the scene.

"Put out a BOLO for those SUVs," Dean ordered one of the deputies as he ran for his patrol unit.

It seemed like mere seconds had passed when a ranch truck driven by one of the hands pulled up as well. A handful of men jumped out and hurried over.

"They took off in a couple of black SUVs. Not sure we can overtake them, but we can try." Beau was telling the hands what had happened in brief, broken sentences.

A tall, skinny hand named Payne Walters shook his head. "You'd better stay with the ladies. We'll see if we can catch up with the shooters."

Sheriff Sharum nodded. "We need to get you back to the house. I'll follow."

When they reached the driveway, Beau spoke briefly to Dean as they got out of their vehicles. "I'm not sure who this guy is, but he seems to have some far-reaching influence."

"You're sure she's telling the truth?" Dean assessed his expression carefully.

Beau didn't hesitate. "Yes. I have no reason to doubt what she's told me."

But his gut seized in sudden argument. Didn't he have reason to doubt? His instincts told him everything wasn't quite what it seemed. But how did Evie play into that?

"If you trust her, I trust her." Dean smiled in assurance. "We'll figure this out."

He pulled away with the promise to let Beau know what they found as soon as he could. Beau didn't expect them to catch up with the shooters, though. Even if they did, he didn't think they would learn anything new. Their attackers were professionals. He had no doubt they would reveal very little, if anything at all.

He went inside to find Evie alone. She looked badly shaken and in need of some fortification. He found he wanted to be the one to hold her up.

He dismissed the thought. "Where's Mia?"

Evie looked up at him with a start. She had apparently been lost in thought and didn't hear him come in. "She went up to her room for a bit."

Beau approached her slowly, as if he was trying to get close to a frightened animal. "Are you okay?"

She had her arms crossed over her chest. "Yeah, I'm fine."

He shook his head. "You don't seem fine."

She turned her eyes on him and looked at him for a long moment. "I've put Mia in a great deal of danger. And there isn't anything I can do about it. She has no one else."

Beau wanted to sympathize with her. But

something told him she needed strength more than sympathy at the moment. “And what about you? You’re in danger, too. But you’re wrong that neither of you have anyone else. You have me. I’m not going to leave you to fight this on your own.”

Evie gave him a look of surprise. “But why? We don’t mean anything to you.”

“You’re wrong there. Neighbors help neighbors around here.” He held out a hand to her.

She took it, and he found her hand felt soft and small in his. “Thank you. I don’t know how I’ll ever repay you for such a gesture.”

“It’s not about repayment. Just doing what’s right.” Beau released her hand, but not before giving it a little squeeze.

She studied him for a moment. “Am I wrong in assuming you know what it’s like to put others in danger? You were an Army Ranger, so I know you’re no stranger to dangerous situations.”

His face contorted into a pained expression. His eyes went dark. For a moment she thought he would tell her to mind her own business. But when he answered, her breath caught.

“You heard me telling your sister I learned to fly before becoming a paratrooper? Well, I didn’t just decide I would rather parachute. I gave up flying because I couldn’t do it anymore." Beau squeezed his eyes shut, but not before she saw the sheen in the blue depths.

She didn't think he was going to continue. "I'm sorry. I shouldn't have asked something so personal."

He shook his head. "No. Maybe it's time I talk about it. I was flying one day on a test run with one of the best friends I had made in the army. His name was Canaan Ledger. I was dating his sister, pretty seriously, actually. But somehow, we managed to stay close. Something went wrong with the plane. I thought I had checked all the controls thoroughly, but I must have missed something. We both bailed, but he got hung up on the way down. His parachute got stuck in a tree, and it strangled him before anyone could get to him."

His voice sounded strained. But he continued despite the tears in Evie's eyes. "The army said it wasn't my fault. Declared it equipment failure. But I know I must've missed something. He left a wife behind. I never flew a plane again."

Evie put the back of her hand to her mouth, the horror of what he must have felt sinking in as he finished the story. "Did his sister blame you?"

He shook his head, eyes fixed somewhere in the past. "No. She said it wasn't my fault, that for whatever unfair reason, God had decided it was just Canaan's time to go. But I couldn't let it go so easily. When I looked at her, all I could see was Canaan's face. So I broke things off. She's happily married now, and I've moved on. I'm glad she's happy. I just never got over Canaan's death."

"What a horrible thing for their family to have to endure. And you as well. I'm so sorry, Beau." She laid a hand over the top of his.

Mia came down the stairs then, interrupting the moment. "Evie, I'm hungry."

Evie nodded, swallowing back the sorrow of what Beau had just shared with her. "Oh, yes, it's past time for something to eat. Let me see what I can find for all of us."

As she disappeared into the kitchen, Beau fought back the storm of tender emotions that swelled within him just then. The comfort Evie had offered him came closer to breaking down his walls than anything he had experienced in the past few years. He didn't know how to handle that.

One thing he was acutely aware of, however. He could sure get used to seeing Evie in his home caring for them all, and Mia smiling down at him like she knew a secret.

It almost made his resolve to stay a bachelor crumble right then and there.

* * *

Evie's hands were shaking as she pulled ingredients for a quick meal from the cabinets in Beau's kitchen. His words kept echoing back to her, the kindness and concern in them, and his promise that he was there for them warmed her thoroughly. Yet she knew she had to stop reacting to Beau like this. Falling for a man got her into this situation to begin with. Following her emotions didn't ever turn out well, and she couldn't make an exception in Beau's case, no matter how wonderful he might be.

She tried to focus on the task at hand, pulling together a salad and some toasted club sandwiches. He had a large, well-laid-out kitchen with industrial-sized appliances and plenty of workspace. It was a chef's dream. The ingredients were easy to find, and she cleaned up as she went. She was laying it all out on the table when a knock came at the door in the living room. She paused to listen and heard Beau reply.

"Yes, she's here. What is this about?"

The answering words were muffled, but her hands began to shake anew. Beau's tone had sounded defensive. She should probably go into the living room and see what was going on, but the rolling in her stomach held her back. Something about this didn't feel right.

Beau came into the kitchen a minute later with a grim expression. "Evie, there are some detectives here. They want to question you about Ruark's murder."

She felt violently ill. She had known this could happen. Didn't they always question the spouse or romantic partner first? Even though they had broken up months before, she might still look suspicious to the law. She tried to nod, but it only succeeded in making her feel dizzy. "Will I have to go to the police station?"

Her voice sounded like someone else talking. But she had to know. The thought of being taken into custody terrified her. She closed her eyes and tried to steady herself. She felt Beau's hand close gently over hers.

"I don't think so. This is just preliminary questioning. I believe they have to have evidence against you to take you in." Beau paused, searching her face. "And I'll be right here with you."

She nodded, but dread pooled in her stomach. She felt numb with shock. How was she supposed to answer their questions when she could hardly breathe?

She allowed Beau to lead her into the living room and help her sit down. The two men waiting there looked anything but friendly.

One of the men spoke as she sat. "Ms. Langston. My name is Detective Hardin, and this is Detective Benton. We need to ask you a few questions concerning the murder of Ruark Beaty."

She could do no more than nod. She pressed her hands together and wedged them in between her knees. Maybe it would steady her quaking just a bit.

"We understand you were in a romantic relationship with Beaty?" The same detective spoke.

"Not recently, no. We dated for a while but haven't been together for over eight months." She found her voice sounded weak but couldn't seem to force it into being stronger.

The two men exchanged a glance before the one identified as Detective Benton wrote something down in a small notebook. Hardin spoke again.

"And did the relationship end amicably?"

Evie drew a deep breath. "As amicably as a breakup could be, I suppose. He often tried to contact me, hoping to get back together. But I had seen his true colors and wanted no part of it."

Benton spoke now. "What do you mean by that? What 'true colors' are you referring to?"

"He seemed the dishonest type. He had some friends that weren't exactly on good terms with the law." Evie wanted to squirm, but she held still. It would only make her look guilty.

"Can you elaborate on that statement?" Hardin's expression was one of annoyance.

Evie thought for a moment on how to word her next statement. "I learned after we broke up that he had dealings with a man named Rich White. I heard rumors recently that he had stolen money from him. I didn't doubt the truth of that, considering that shortly before we ended our relationship, he quit his job. But he seemed to be spending more money than ever. It was suspicious behavior."

Benton was taking down more notes, and Hardin stepped closer. "And you claim you knew nothing about his involvement with Rich White before your breakup?"

Evie shook her head. "I did not."

"And you also knew nothing about the home he bought in the Caribbean?" Hardin fixed her with a hard stare.

"Absolutely not." Evie was stunned.

"So we are to believe you dated a man for a while but you knew nothing about his illegal activities?" Hardin raised his voice.

"I did not. I worked a great deal. I saw him on weekends and occasionally on evenings throughout the week. We had separate homes and didn't spend a great deal of time together."

Evie realized now how pathetic their relationship had been. Ruark had certainly played her for a fool.

Benton spoke up again. "Where is it that you worked during this time, Ms. Langston? We know that you are currently self-employed."

"I worked for a company called Harbinger Mays. I have a degree in agriculture and minors in psychology and counseling." Evie wasn't sure why she felt the need to include this last, but maybe it would lend some credibility to her words.

"Why did you leave? Wyoming is a long way from Oklahoma." Benton again.

"I plan to start an equine rehabilitation therapy center. It's been a lifelong dream of mine, and I finally saved up sufficient funds. This seemed like the place to start my business, since it was the best deal I could find on the real estate, and horses generally aren't difficult to find in Wyoming." She finally got the nerve to glance at Beau. His expression was inscrutable, however. He looked more intimidating than she had ever seen him. Was he doubting her innocence? This last admission certainly made it look like she had come into some money. Would they believe she had merely saved it up?

"It's convenient that you have the funds now

that Beaty is dead." Hardin's voice oozed with sarcasm, confirming her fears.

"I've been saving for this since I was nineteen. And I have applied for grants as well as a loan to help me get started." Evie ignored his sarcasm. Benton shot his partner a look.

"That's easily verified." Hardin gave Benton a nod, presumably to make a note to check her facts on this.

"I would be glad to have you verify it. I have nothing to hide." Evie sat as still as she could.

"You realize from where we are sitting, we have cause to doubt your innocence in Ruark Beaty's murder." Hardin was going in for the kill. Maybe he thought he would frighten her into a confession.

"I didn't kill him. I haven't even seen him in months." Evie looked Detective Hardin in the eye.

He stared back for a moment before finally turning away with a sigh. "We'll be watching you very closely, Ms. Langston. Don't go anywhere. Once we have checked your financials and verified your statement, you can expect to hear from us again."

He motioned to Benton, who followed him out.

Once the door shut behind them, Evie crumpled. "They don't believe me. They really think I killed him."

Beau moved over to the sofa to sit down beside her. "Once they check out your facts, maybe they will move on."

Evie worried that was unlikely. From where those detectives stood, she did look guilty.

And she wasn't sure how to prove her innocence.

SIX

Beau didn't know what to think. Evie certainly didn't seem like the type to commit murder. But she had left the state. She was starting a business with a lot of money. And he had only known her a couple of days. How much faith could he put into someone in a situation like that? It didn't help that she wasn't meeting his eyes. Maybe from embarrassment, but it could be out of guilt.

He would need to pray about this.

Mia, thankfully, had stayed in her room while the detectives were there. When Evie called her down, it looked like she had been sleeping.

"What took so long?" Mia yawned, digging into her sandwich.

Evie looked in his direction. "Things came up. I'm sorry you had to wait."

Mia didn't ask what, though Beau had expected her to. He began to eat his own sandwich, but noticed Evie barely nibbled at hers.

He should get her mind off it. "This is delicious. Makes me glad you're going to be cooking for us."

She looked up from her salad. "I'm glad you like it."

He was going to have to try something else. "What do you plan to work on first at your ranch? You must be anxious to get the therapy center up and running." Beau glanced at Mia, who was still eating with gusto.

"I want to get the barns repaired and locate some good horses. The arena's in pretty good shape, but some of the turn-out paddock fences might need work." Evie stirred the salad with her fork.

"What about the house? Don't you want to make it a little more livable before you do all the work out there?" Beau was shaking his head. She was unlike any woman he had met.

"It's not a priority." She finally took a bite.

"I think Mia might disagree. And the house is the first impression your clients will get of your facilities. Do you think it'll make a good one?" Beau was trying not to grin.

Mia snickered. They all knew it wouldn't.

Evie chewed thoughtfully. "I hadn't thought of that."

They got no further when a beeping told Beau he had received a new message on his phone. A glance revealed it was Dean Sharum.

He looked up at Evie. "I'm going to go make a phone call. Be right back."

She simply nodded, still looking quite pale. Mia didn't even look up from her sandwich.

A few minutes later, Dean was on the phone, telling him that their attackers from the shed seemed to have completely disappeared. "We suspect they must have a hideout close by. I have men searching for it. We're doing everything we can."

"I appreciate it. But we have another problem." Beau told him about the detectives showing up to question Evie.

"I know you believe she's innocent, and after meeting her, I'd have a tough time believing her capable of murder as well. But I've been surprised before. Be careful." Dean sounded sympathetic.

"I will. Let me know if you find anything else." Beau waited for Dean's affirmation then disconnected.

His friend was right. People did have a way of surprising you. It just reminded him he had to keep his guard up.

After all, there were no guarantees in life. He had finally found someone he could trust and confide in with Caitlyn, and things had gone horribly wrong. He knew none of it was her fault, and he had been the one to break it off. But before he could work through his trauma and consider giving it another chance, she was with someone new.

It was the cruel fact of life that sometimes people were taken from this earth earlier than others. He missed Canaan every day and knew he'd not been the same since his death. It wasn't until after the breakup, when he heard Caitlyn was engaged, that he learned she had met the new man before she had even separated from Beau. She denied any relationship with her new fiancé before that point, but Beau had heard rumors that said otherwise.

And no matter what he might be feeling for Evie right now, not only was he afraid to risk losing someone else, but he didn't want to hurt Evie either.

Evie sensed something had changed with Beau.

She knew the detectives showing up to question her would complicate things, but it was something more than that. He had grown distant after the phone call from his sheriff friend.

Beau waited until Mia had gone back up to

her room to read a book before explaining what the sheriff's patrol had encountered.

"So they are probably just hired hit men?" Evie asked.

"It looks like it. But if they could question them, maybe we could get closer to ending this." Beau didn't say more.

"I don't understand why they can't just arrest Rich White and be done with it. Surely they have some reason." Evie knew she was oversimplifying things, but she was tired and just wanted it to end.

"You know it isn't that easy. They need evidence to convict him of anything serious." Beau's voice was patient, but she knew he was weary of this as well.

"Yes, I do. I'm sorry. Maybe I should be more like Mia. She doesn't seem to be letting any of this affect her at all." Evie rose to clean up the table.

"It's a little more personal for you. And I'm sure it's affecting her more than you know. She just isn't showing it." Beau took the plates from her and rinsed them in the sink before putting them in the dishwasher.

His thoughtful gesture softened her heart toward him just a little, despite her mental protests.

"I'm sure you're right. It's not an easy situation to find yourself in." Evie wiped down the table, and when everything was done, she turned to face him. "I need to go check on Harvey. He's happy nosing around outside, but I should check his food and water."

The scruffy little rescue dog seemed to be content to be where Mia was. However, she seemed to have forgotten about him in all the excitement.

Beau glanced out the kitchen window. "Okay. Dean has patrols passing by every so often, so it should be fine. Just stay alert. I need to check on the hands as well. I'll be at the barn if you need anything."

Evie walked out the front door and onto the porch, calling for Harvey. The little dog came running, tail wagging happily. She rubbed behind his ears and spoke softly to him before replenishing his food and water. When he was enthusiastically lapping up water, she turned toward the barn. She didn't really want to return to the house just yet. It was a beautiful afternoon, and she hated to waste it indoors.

She had just turned the corner, however, when a shadow caught her eye just beyond a tree to her left. She turned, thinking it was just an animal or a shadow from a bird passing overhead. She didn't see anything else, so she kept walking. Maybe she was just being paranoid, jumping at every shadow.

The barn was a couple dozen more yards away, so she kept watch as she strode across the open space between the buildings. Harvey ran up behind her, startling her.

Her heart thumped recklessly in her chest, so she gave herself a good talking to. *Get a grip, Evie. You're perfectly safe. Stop being afraid of everything.*

She stopped to pet Harvey one more time until he stopped wiggling under her touch and jumped up to race after a butterfly. She smiled, watching him. She longed to be so carefree herself.

Evie decided to bypass the barn for the time being and lean against the corral to watch a couple of Beau's horses chasing each other playfully. Her thoughts wouldn't settle, however, so she wandered back toward the barn. She rounded a corner and almost tripped over Harvey.

He was growling at something.

Her eyes moved upward then and discovered exactly what had him agitated.

The nose of a 9 mm was pointed at her from just a few feet away.

SEVEN

"Call off your dog." The voice behind the gun was quiet but demanding.

Evie nervously complied. "Harvey, down boy."

She wasn't sure if he would obey, but he did. He sniffed the ground near where they stood, however, whining in displeasure. With a pang, she realized she had forgotten her Smith & Wesson that Beau had warned her to always carry. Not that it would have done her much good now, anyway.

"Now walk. Quickly, before someone sees. There's no one in that foaling shed over there. I've already checked it out. Move." There was no room for argument in the gunman's tone. He wore a black bandanna over his head, dark sunglasses and had a full dark beard. Evie noted a large tattoo on the hand that held the gun on her as well. She wasn't certain what it was, but it gave her the creeps.

She didn't have time to dwell on the tattoo, however. She made her way to the shed where he directed her, trying to walk as slowly as possible without angering him further in hopes that someone might appear to help her.

No one did. They reached the shed, and he closed the doors and barred them from the inside. What did he plan to do with her here?

He shoved his gun in his waistband and tied her wrists. His actions sent her blood into a cold spiral then. "I understand you don't want to give up the money, and you don't want to come peacefully. That's where I come in. I'm the guy who knows how to make people talk. Richie keeps me on for just that purpose. I can get in, get answers, and get out."

He held up an evil-looking knife with a vicious, curved blade that came to a sharp point. "Where shall we start?"

"Please." Evie whispered the words as he forced her to sit on the ground.

He tied her ankles and chuckled. "I haven't even started yet. Most don't beg for mercy until I start to work."

"But I'm telling the truth. I don't know anything about the money. It was Ruark. He didn't tell me anything about it." Evie fought to keep her calm. What could she do to convince him?

He put his face very close to hers. "I don't believe you."

She struggled, knowing even beforehand it was futile. This wasn't some hired thug. He was on the payroll of a very bad man, a man whom no one seemed to be able to catch up with. Evie had never met him, but she had heard stories and news reports of crimes thought to be related to his gangs. He was horrible.

She expected nothing less from this guy.

All she could do was pray. *Lord, please send me some help here. You know the degree of my innocence. I don't know what to do.*

Her lips moved, though she said the words to herself, not wanting to give this man further ammunition of any kind. He still noticed.

"That's right, go ahead and pray. It isn't going to help you. Talk!" He shouted this last word.

"I dated Ruark for a few months. I broke up with him when he started acting strangely, and he tried for months to get me to take him back. It wasn't until recently that I learned he had stolen money from your boss. I haven't spoken to him in eight months." Her voice sounded high-pitched and rushed, but there was nothing she could do about it. Her nerves were on edge.

"That's a nice story." He held the knife up close again. "Where should I start?"

He wiggled the knife around in a serpentine pattern just above her face, chest, and neck, making a face of concentration. Then he pointed the tip of it at her throat. "Most people need a little convincing that I'm serious."

The razor-sharp tip of the knife pricked the sensitive skin in the hollow of her throat and she gasped. "I believe you're serious. I can tell you where Ruark banked, where he hung out and where he lived. But he never told me anything about stealing any money."

"Those things might help if we didn't already know all that. Don't you think Richie has checked all that out? There's no money. What about you? Where do you bank? That's what we need to check out."

Evie closed her eyes, sending up another silent prayer. *Please help me, Lord.* She was careful not to move her lips this time. "Go ahead. But I thought you already knew all that information. If you have Ruark's information, you must have mine as well."

Instead of getting angry at her words, he leaned closer with an evil smile. He poised the knife against her skin once more, this time next to her cheek. "I find most people are pretty vain when it comes to having their faces scarred up. Especially ladies."

Evie sucked in a breath, the sharp point resting uncomfortably against the high part of her cheekbone. The knife-wielding man gave out a nasty chuckle. "I used to want to be a surgeon. Working for Richie pays better. And I don't have to worry about my knife slipping."

He was startled then by the rattling of the barred doors of the shed. His knife slipped just before he jerked it back on instinct. Evie could feel a trickle of blood winding down her cheek just below the stinging wound.

A shout came from the other side of the doors, followed by pounding. "Evie, are you in there?"

Harvey was barking incessantly, too. That wonderful little dog was trying to save her. She tried to shout a reply, but her captor's hand snaked over her mouth just in time to muffle her shout.

It was enough, though. "Let her go!" Beau shouted.

Her captor didn't reply, eyes searching the darkened shed for any avenue of escape. He had dropped the knife, thankfully, and was dragging her as far away from the door as he could. Her hands and ankles were still tied, so she felt the scrape of the dirt and shavings beneath her as he pulled her upright enough to hold on to her. Her bound ankles had made it impossible to do more than let herself be pulled along.

Beau hadn't said any more, but Harvey still barked threateningly on the other side of the door. It wasn't long before she heard a new sound. A deep rhythmic thudding indicated he was hitting the door of the shed with something very heavy.

Her captor cursed. He was almost frantic now, looking around him still for anything to help his cause. Evie struggled with all her might trying to get free of his terrible grip. She managed to loosen an elbow enough to plant it in his nose. He yelped and she screamed.

It was seconds later when a splintering sound echoed through the shed. For a split second, her captor waffled between trying to hang on to her and trying to make his escape. He still held on to her with both hands, so he hadn't drawn his gun. Evie vowed to warn Beau. They could make their move as soon as her captor released her to flee.

"Beau! Gun!" It came out a scream.

She knew her captor would try to run because he had been staring at the single, tiny window on the south side of the shed.

When he shoved her away, Evie was ready, bracing her core so that her weight wouldn't hit the ground so hard in the fall. "He's got a gun!"

She uttered the words as soon as the grunt left her lungs on impact with the ground. Beau was chasing the man across the small space and when he tried to smash out the window, Beau grabbed him by the shirt and pulled him backward.

The two men fell to the ground, wrestling and throwing punches in a melee that had Evie's head spinning. Harvey had run into the shed as well and had the man by the pant leg, growling and snarling the whole while. The man tried to shake him off, but he was too busy dealing with the fierce blows Beau was raining down on his head.

Evie noticed Beau's phone had wriggled out of his back pocket and she grabbed for it, awkwardly positioning her hands so that she could call 911 as fast as she could.

By the time she had finished with the dispatcher, however, the other man had gained the advantage. He had pulled his gun and held it on Beau, then pointed it at Evie.

"Not another move, either of you. I'm going, but Richie always gets his money." He ducked out the splintered door and fled, Harvey on his heels.

"Harvey!" Evie called, not wanting the little dog to get hurt.

Beau struggled to his feet. He was losing his edge. How did that guy get the drop on him?

He glanced at Evie. "I promise I'll be right back. And I'll get Harvey." Beau shouted the words at her as he ran after him.

"Go! Catch him. I'm fine." He barely registered her brave words as he pursued the man. The sight of the dust clinging to the caked rivulet of blood on her cheek and neck was doing uncomfortable things to the pit of his stomach, and he wanted this guy to pay.

But when he ran out of the shed, all he could see was a flash of dark clothing as the man bolted around the corner of the main barn. He was fast, Beau had to give him that.

"Payne! Sawyer! I need some help!" He shouted at the hands as he ran by the open barn door.

The two men emerged, but it was too late. Evie's attacker was long gone.

"What's going on?" Payne spoke first.

Beau only pointed at the dark figure disappearing from view, his breathing labored. "Someone attacked Evie."

"Where is she?" Sawyer asked.

"Still in the foaling shed. He had her bound at the wrists and ankles." Beau led the way back to the shed.

The ranch hands helped him loosen her bonds as she told them what had happened. Beau couldn't suppress his anger that the man had gotten to her right under their very noses. "We have to be more vigilant. How did he get onto the property without anyone noticing?"

The hands eyed each other guiltily. "We were just busy, and I guess no one noticed. We aren't used to having to worry about that sort of thing." It was Sawyer who said this.

"We'll keep a closer eye out from now on, though. I feel terrible that this happened." Payne was looking at the dried blood on Evie's face and throat.

Evie was looking embarrassed. She seemed even more pale against the crimson splotches. "I should've been more careful."

She bent down and Harvey flew into her arms. She ruffed his fur and hugged him as she praised the wriggling little dog. "What a good boy you are, Harvey. You saved me."

"We all should've been more careful. Come on. Let's go get you cleaned up." Beau's anger was subsiding but only a little bit.

The hands went back to work, promising to keep a better watch, and Beau led Evie from the shed, eyes scanning for further danger the whole while.

Mia was coming down the stairs when they walked into the house. She gasped when she saw Evie. It was bad timing for sure.

"I'm fine, Mia. Just fine." Evie smiled weakly, but her voice was strong.

"What happened?" Mia wanted to know.

Evie hesitated, mouth opening and closing again.

Beau took over for her. "A man snuck onto the property and grabbed her. We need to be very careful not to go anywhere alone."

Mia needed to know there was danger. He understood that Evie wanted to shield her, but Beau felt it would do more harm than good not to be up front with Mia in this case.

"Oh, man!" Mia hurried the rest of the way down the steps to reach Evie's side. "He cut you?"

Evie simply nodded, looking to Beau once more.

"Mia, I need to get some things to clean up these cuts. She might need stitches. Can you stay with her?" Beau settled Mia beside Evie on the sofa.

"I won't leave her. I promise." Mia gave him a nod.

Beau went to gather the things he needed, thinking the whole while about Mia and Evie. The pair was getting under his skin, and he didn't know what to do about it. Mia was so endearing with her old soul and childish bravado. And Evie… Well, Evie was a gentle soul that called out to him. Her need for protection made it worse. Yes, she was beautiful with her sun-streaked blond hair and wide violet eyes, but it was something deeper that tugged at him. She had a goodness about her he couldn't define.

He swept the thoughts aside as he returned to the living room to find Evie fussing at Mia about needing to be careful and Mia rolling her eyes in response to Evie's words.

"I'm not a baby. I know I need to be careful. Maybe you should listen to your own advice." Mia crossed her arms.

"I didn't say you were," Evie shot back, but then her tone softened. "And you're right. I should be more careful."

They hadn't noticed he was back, and Mia was opening her mouth to say something else when he cleared his throat. "Thank you, Mia."

She scooted over to allow him to get closer to Evie. "What are you going to clean it with?"

Evie fell silent watching the two as Beau explained to her how the antiseptic cleaner would help get rid of germs so her cuts could heal. He also explained the ointment would help prevent scarring, and Evie wondered if she would have the marks from this attack for the rest of her life. She hoped not. She wasn't typically vain, but she didn't relish the questioning stares and the constant reminder of her foolishness in trusting Ruark.

Mia finally grew bored and skipped off to the kitchen, declaring her need for a snack. Once she was out of earshot, Beau fixed a steady gaze on Evie.

"I'm sorry this happened. I don't want you to go anywhere alone. I know it's not easy, but your safety is too important." He glanced toward the kitchen. "You and Mia both need to stay with me any time you leave the house. If Harvey hadn't come to get me, who knows when I would have realized what had happened."

Evie just nodded. Her face was pale, and he knew she was probably still reliving what had just happened in her mind.

"Try not to think about it." He gave the advice, knowing it was easier said than achieved. Then a thought came to him. "I tell you what. I'll check in with the sheriff, and then if the coast is clear, we will all go to the barn together. I'll introduce you to the hands and the horses and tell you about our operation."

"Okay. That would be nice. I don't want to just sit around thinking about the attack, for sure." Evie was frowning as she confirmed his suspicions.

"Give me a few minutes." Beau took out his

cell phone and stepped out onto the porch. He called Dean Sharum's personal phone and told him what had just happened.

He echoed Beau's sentiments about Harvey. "That little dog might have saved her life. I would keep him close. I'll see what I can do about stepping up patrols around your place, but we are terribly shorthanded right now. It's becoming a bit of a crisis. Just keep close watch and have your men do the same."

"Will do. Thank you." Beau hesitated, but the detectives questioning Evie still bothered him. "Did you learn anything else about why the detectives were questioning Evie about the murder?"

"Not so far. But you know it isn't unusual to suspect the ex-girlfriend, wife, or significant other first." Dean cleared his throat on the other end of the line. "Does she have any motive?"

"I don't know what it would be." Beau knew the detectives probably wouldn't see it that way, though. If he had stolen money, they would think she wanted it for herself. He couldn't see that from Evie, though.

Was he being blind? Something about her made him want to trust her, though trust wasn't something he gave out easily. He couldn't pinpoint why Evie would be different. He sensed a goodness beneath her outer shell, something deeper than just her words that made him think she was trustworthy.

But he couldn't repeat what he went through with Caitlyn. If he got attached to Evie and something else like that happened, he couldn't take it.

He had to keep her at a distance, even if it was the last thing he wanted to do.

EIGHT

Evie followed Beau and Mia out to the stable a little while later, but her heart now beat so hard she could hear it echoing in her ears. She took in the yard and all the corrals surrounding the barns, as well as looking behind her frequently. Harvey came loping up to join them as soon as he noticed they were outside and she reached down to pat him on the head, still praising him for being a good boy.

The stable was amazingly clean, with concrete floors in the aisles, cross ties between the stalls for grooming, and meticulously maintained pine slat stalls with bars at the top. The scent of freshly spread pine shavings welcomed them, and a couple of the horses stuck their heads over the doors of their stalls, wide brown eyes curious about their visitors. Their shining coats gleamed in the well-lit space. Mia was already gasping and oohing over the horses, asking Beau questions about them as they went.

"Careful, Mia. Don't startle them," Evie cautioned her little sister as she gestured wildly with her hands.

"I've been around horses before, Evie. I even went on a trail ride with a friend once." Mia puffed up like this made her an authority.

"Trail horses are a little different from ranch horses, though. Ranches who offer trail rides carefully choose gentle horses that aren't easily spooked and are very forgiving to inexperienced riders. These horses have a different job," Evie explained.

"What's their job? Chasing cows?" Mia asked. She looked at Beau.

"Sometimes. These horses are expert cutters, roping horses and reiners. When we need to move or doctor cattle, we still use horses to bring them into the corrals. Once they're there, we can run them through that narrow chute you saw outside, hold on to them by their heads with a pair of movable metal bars called a head chute and give them shots, wormers, or whatever they might need to keep them healthy." Beau was stroking the nose of a beautiful bay horse next to him as he explained.

"But why does that mean they can't be gentle?" Mia reached over to stroke the horse's nose as well when Beau nodded, indicating it was okay.

"They can be. This is Taz and he's pretty gentle. But most cow horses are accustomed to certain types of riders. Cowboys and cowgirls that know how to ride very well and don't make mistakes in the saddle. There are a lot of specific cues a rider can give with their hands and feet, and many beginners might give those cues on accident, confusing the horse. Young horses don't know how to respond to that sometimes, and it frustrates them. It can be dangerous." Beau gave the horse a pat on the vivid white star in the middle of his forehead.

"So Evie isn't gonna get horses like these for her therapy center." Mia looked put out by the fact.

"Definitely not." Evie grinned. "These horses are way too expensive for my needs anyway."

Beau chuckled at Mia's pout. "Tell you what. You take some riding lessons and when you get good enough, I'll teach you to ride a real cow horse myself."

Evie swallowed hard. Did he realize what he was saying? That he wanted to be a part of their lives far into the future? She felt a little queasy at the thought. He was giving her butterflies, but saying things like that...

He probably hadn't meant it like her poor battered heart was taking it, of course. They would be neighbors far into the future. But it was still overwhelming to think about. She shouldn't be having these feelings for a man at all.

Beau must have asked her a question because he and Mia both were looking at her expectantly. He looked mildly amused.

"I'm sorry. I was lost in thought." And her face heated thinking about what had made her so distracted.

"No problem. I just asked where you planned to find your therapy horses." Beau smiled lazily before turning back to the horse beside him. Taz tossed his head playfully as Beau rubbed the star once more.

"I don't really know yet. I have looked into a couple of sales, but they all seem to have fancier horses than what I need." Evie shook her head. It had been a frustrating search, honestly.

"What about rescue horses?" Beau asked, turning back to look her in the eye. "Some are a little rough around the edges, but many of them are just older horses that need a good home."

"That sounds like just what I need. How do I find them?" Evie felt a little bubble of hope at the thought.

"There is a local rescue organization that could help you out. Maybe even get you some of the horses you need for a small adoption fee just to be sure they got a good home. Dean Sharum's wife, Whitney, heads it up." Beau walked down to the next stall. "I could arrange for you to meet with her if you like."

Evie felt the grin spread across her face, and when she looked at Mia, she could tell her sister wasn't completely put off by the idea either. "That would be wonderful."

He nodded and they walked on through the stable. Beau introduced them to all the horses in the barn, explaining which ones were gentle, which were crabby and even one that tended to bite. Mia took a step back immediately when Beau introduced Stitch as a biter.

"Like the movie, *Lilo and Stitch*?" Mia giggled.

"Exactly like that Stitch. Except this is a mare. But she was named after that character for a reason. She's a handful."

Evie laughed, too. She watched as the little mare pinned her ears back against her head and nipped at Beau. He chastised her and motioned for them to go to the next stall. Maudie, Earp and Frankie all greeted them politely. Simba sniffed around for a treat, making Mia laugh delightedly when Beau gave her one to feed him.

"Hold your hand flat so he can get hold of the treat, not your fingers," Beau instructed her, but when Evie looked at him, he was looking at her, not Mia. Her heart switched up its rhythm again.

Harvey gave a little bark, startling her out of her thoughts. He had been on her heels the whole time, and though she was grateful for his protection, she had almost forgotten he was there. “What is it, buddy?”

He growled low, and Beau came to attention. “Is someone there?”

A clatter sounded at the other end of the barn, and a young man in a straw cowboy hat sauntered out, holding up a clanging mélange of leather straps. “It’s just me, boss. I needed another bridle. Mine snapped.”

“No problem, Tory. This is Evie, and her sister, Mia.” Beau made a quick introduction, and the cowhand tipped his hat to each of them.

“Nice to meet you.” He grinned. “Sorry for the fright.”

He disappeared and Evie gave a sigh of relief. “I hate living in fear like this.”

She said it low and close to Beau’s ear, hoping Mia wouldn’t hear. He didn’t respond, just pressed his lips into a firm line. Harvey leaned close into her leg, though, still at alert.

“It’s okay, boy. He’s a friend.” Evie scratched behind his ears, but the little dog didn’t relax.

"Beau?" Evie looked at him, feeling like something was still off.

A flash from outside the door of the barn caught his attention.

One of the hands shouted from the corral.

Evie felt a prickle at the back of her neck just as Harvey let out a vicious bark.

"Stay here. You and Mia lock yourselves into the tack room and don't come out until I come and get you." Beau peeked inside the room he indicated to be sure it was safe, then motioned them inside.

Once inside, Evie locked the door and leaned against it, facing Mia. Her sister sat down on the concrete floor. Evie watched her for a moment, wishing there was something she could do to reassure her sister.

What had she gotten them into?

Beau made sure the females were safely locked in the tack room and ran for the door of the barn. He had stashed his 9 mm in the holster, and he pulled it out as he went. Two of the hands were already running toward the shed where Beau had seen the light glint across the metal of a gun.

A ping hit the side of the barn. A warning shot?

His mind was going as fast as his legs. If

they wanted the money and thought Evie had it, why would they be shooting? Was he their target since he was protecting her? Or did the gunman just intend to get closer and use the gun for coercion purposes?

Either way, Beau was tired of these guys getting onto his property unchecked. He holstered his gun and ran after him.

He overtook the two hands, catching a flash of dark clothing as the guy with the gun ducked from behind one shed to another barn. Beau dug deep and pulled out a little more speed.

"Stop!" He barked the command as the dark-clad gunman came into view once more.

He could hear the cowhands running behind him and he pushed a little harder, almost reaching the other man as he dived toward a line of trees along the property. Beau stumbled as he reached for the intruder, almost getting tangled in some low brush. He shook free and continued after him, so close he could hear the man's labored breathing.

The man turned for just a second, but his face was shrouded in a ski mask, and all Beau could make out was dark eyes staring back at him. The shadows from the trees danced over the man as he bolted that much harder away from Beau. He was medium height and thin in build. It made him fast, and Beau had to push to keep up.

Just when Beau thought he was going to slip away, the man stumbled over Harvey, who had come to help, and Beau had his chance. He dived at the man, taking advantage of the fact that he was off balance, and knocking him to the ground. They tussled about in the overgrowth for a few minutes. Beau swung an arm out at the man, causing him to lose hold of his gun. The wiry man was quick and hard to keep hold of, just slipping out of his grip several times. Frustration redoubled Beau's efforts, and he battled hard to keep the man from getting away. Harvey barked furiously, but thankfully stayed out of the way.

Beau finally managed to get in a good solid blow. He whisked his dropped gun off into the brush where the other man couldn't easily retrieve it while the other man tried to shake off the stunning punch. Beau pulled out his own Glock on the man as Tory and Payne crashed through the thicket. Beau aimed the Glock at the other man and stared him down. Harvey stood sentry beside him, his attention on their captive.

The dark-clad man cursed.

"Keep an eye on him, boss. A deputy is on the way," Payne told him. "Sawyer called it in."

"Meanwhile, who is this fella?" Tory moved closer, intending to pull off the ski mask that covered the man's face. The man ducked away for a moment, catching Tory's hand and knocking it away, until Beau reminded him a gun was aimed at him.

Tory smirked at the guy and pulled off the mask. Dark eyes stared back at them from an angry, mean looking brow. "Anybody know this guy?"

Beau didn't, so he shook his head and looked at the others. He felt like he was a bit familiar, but he didn't know how or why. "No. I don't think I do. Payne?"

The cowhand shook his head slowly, but he had the same look of consternation Beau felt on his own face. "No, not exactly."

They didn't have further chance to reason it out before a whoop of a patrol car's siren let them know the deputy had arrived. When he reached the men, the lawman cuffed the intruder and prepared to put him in the patrol car.

"Wait, you can't arrest me. I didn't do anything. You don't even know that gun was mine." The man was protesting to the deputy. Evie's attacker hadn't been able to retrieve his gun, and though Beau showed the deputy where it was, it wasn't on his person.

"Trespassing. And the word of Mr. Thorpe. That's good enough around here." The deputy shoved him in the car.

"Can you hold him on anything?" Beau asked the question once the car door closed on the man.

"Not for long. I'm sure they'll post bail. We'll do our best to make him talk, though."

The deputy nodded and got into his car.

Beau ran a hand through his hair and sighed before going back to tell the girls it was safe. The two hands followed him, and Sawyer joined them as they neared the stable. When Beau got back to the tack room, he knocked on the door and told the females it was safe to come out. Evie swung open the door and stared at Beau and the three cowhands.

"He got away?" She was as pale as ever. Mia sat behind her.

"No, they took him in for questioning, but I didn't recognize him. Just another of White's hired thugs, I suppose." He shook his head.

"Do you think he's gonna try to stick to his story? Surely the deputy knew that was his gun." Tory was frowning.

"He tried to deny it?" Evie looked at Beau in concern.

Payne nodded his head. "Yeah, but all the law around here knows the Thorpes. That guy didn't look like anyone I've ever seen in the area. His word won't mean much against Beau's."

Beau sent Payne a look, hoping they would all let it drop. Evie was probably feeling like her word wasn't worth much to anyone after all that had happened recently, and he didn't want to make her feel worse. She gave him a questioning look.

"I'll explain it all later. Right now, we should probably head back to the house." He looked over to see Mia making a pouty face.

"I wanted to meet the rest of the horses." She crossed her arms over her chest.

"Mia," Evie began.

"How about I take her? I was about to take a little break anyway." Payne made the offer while he bent close to Mia. "My name is Payne. My sister says it's because I am one."

That comment elicited a giggle from Mia. "My sister is, too, sometimes."

Evie rolled her eyes. "Are you sure you want to deal with this munchkin?"

Payne smiled. "I think we'll get along just fine."

Evie watched them go, shaking her head. Sawyer and Tory sauntered off after them. Beau waited, knowing the questions were coming.

She started with the one he least expected, however. "What did he mean about your family? I guess you have a long history with the locals?"

Beau looked at the ground. "I guess you could say that. My family has lived here for several generations. I have four brothers. Our whole family has been in law enforcement or military at one point. My older brother Grayson was a US marshal and now works as a security adviser in the White House. My twin brother Briggs was a navy SEAL before retiring to raise buffalo in Oklahoma. Avery worked as a state investigator after a stint as a detective in Cheyenne, though he's now working as a private investigator. Caldwell, the baby, has a law degree, but he ended up working as a state investigator in Texas for a while. I'm not sure what he's doing now."

"What do you mean?" Evie looked confused.

"He went AWOL. Last we heard, he married some girl from Georgia, but none of us have even met her. Caldwell has always been… difficult. I don't know how to explain it. Our mother left us all with our father when we were young, and it affected Caldwell a little differently than the rest of us. She reconciled with most of us, but Caldwell won't come around. It hasn't been easy for any of us." Beau's face clouded as he explained.

"I'm sorry. That must be really tough on all of you." Evie laid a hand on his forearm. He tried to ignore the surge of awareness he felt for her at the simple touch. He forced his mind to focus on something else.

"Why don't we go ahead and give Whitney a call. Maybe we can set up a time for you to look at some horses. Your barn is in decent shape, right? And we should have some extra time around here later this week once we finish moving hay in from the fields. I'll get some of the hands to help me repair your fences. Would you be okay with that?"

"I could pay you, but not much." Evie scrunched up her face.

"I'm not looking for pay. It helps me for the neighboring ranch to have good fences also, you know. We all need to keep our livestock where it belongs." Beau made the comment, hoping she wouldn't consider the fact that the fences on his side of the property were already in good shape. It would be the outer borders that didn't adjoin his property that needed the most work.

The look she gave him indicated she did know this, but she didn't mention it. "Thank you."

He nodded. "I'm not great at roofing, but I could recommend someone who would be reasonable and fair if you want to get to work on the house. Once that's done, I can do just about anything else that needs doing to fix it up. As soon as you're ready, just let me know."

"That would be great." Evie wore a wistful look. Was she thinking of what it would be like to have the pressure of the needed repairs gone?

He pulled up the number to call Whitney Sharum at the rescue facility.

Whitney's mother was a veterinarian, so she helped with making sure the horses were sound and healthy. Some of them were wild, brought in from the surrounding area where the occasional mustang or lost runaway horse roamed free, but several were just rescued from neglectful homes or auctions where they weren't wanted by any but the worst of buyers. He knew it happened, but he hated considering the fate of most elderly, unwanted horses.

"Hi, Whitney, it's Beau Thorpe. I have a new neighbor looking for some horses for a therapy center. She needs some beginner and kid-friendly stock. Do you guys have any animals that might work for that purpose right now?" He glanced at Evie when he mentioned his neighbor.

He had paused to listen to her reply, but then he began to nod before speaking again. "Yes, that sounds like just what she needs. Could we take a look?"

By the time he disconnected, Evie was smiling broadly. "She has some suitable horses?"

Beau smiled back at her. "She says she has at least four that might work. That would be a good start. She said she would keep you in mind if any more became available also."

"Perfect. When can we go?" Evie's enthusiasm was contagious.

"How about tomorrow morning? Is that too soon?" Beau asked.

"Really? I would love to go ahead and go, but will she expect me to take them right then? I still need to fix the fences." Evie wore a surprised expression.

"I'm sure she will be flexible. If you find some horses you like, we can make arrangements to bring them here until your facilities are repaired and ready to go. I have an extra paddock you can keep them in until then." Beau watched her expression turn to amazement, saddened that she would be so unaccustomed to finding kindness in others. It wasn't the first time she had reacted this way.

She lowered her lashes, and just when he thought she might argue, she simply said, "Thank you."

NINE

Evie made a big breakfast the next morning, her childlike excitement giving her an excess of energy. The cowhands filed in as she was settling Mia down with a plate of biscuits, chocolate gravy, bacon and eggs. She heard them whispering but didn't know what it was all about until she turned and saw one cowboy gesturing to the pan of chocolate gravy.

"Oh, I made bacon gravy, too." She reached to pull the pan forward, but another cowboy—Tory, she thought—was shaking his head and laughing.

"What's the matter, boys? Ya'll never seen chocolate gravy before?" He reached in and began to ladle some of the thick, pudding-like gravy onto his biscuits. Sweet, cocoa-scented steam wafted into the air above his plate, scenting the kitchen with its tantalizing aroma.

"They come from different parts, ma'am. Where did you grow up?" Tory asked her.

"I was raised in Oklahoma." She smiled. "What about you?"

"I grew up in Texas, but I lived in Oklahoma for a while also. I worked on a ranch there near Yukon for a while. I also spent some time at a place in Eastern Oklahoma near Checotah." From his expression, she thought he must have fond memories of her state.

"Yes, I know both towns well." Evie nodded.

One by one, the other hands peeked at the substance in the bowl, and, catching the scent, eagerly loaded their biscuits with it. Evie chuckled as they began to taste it and exclaim over how good it was.

Beau was the last man to enter the kitchen, having already been to the barn this morning, and his face lit up at the sight. He grabbed a plate and began filling it up. "I haven't had chocolate gravy in far too long. I'm glad you know how to make it."

"It's really easy, actually. Just cocoa, flour, milk and sugar." Evie blushed.

"It's delicious." Beau winked at her as he tasted a bit from the plate he was making.

However, she found her own appetite was lacking. She was anxious to get going to the rescue center. They had agreed to take Mia, hoping it would help her keep her mind off recent events. So far she had proven very resilient, but Evie thought it would be best not to stretch it too far.

She cleaned up the breakfast dishes as the men made their way out, nibbling a piece of bacon and a small bit of biscuit and gravy. When Beau finally asked if she was ready to go, she had the kitchen back in order and Mia sat in an oversize chair in the living room watching one of her favorite TV shows.

"Mia, are you ready?" Evie was wiping her hands on a dish towel as she called into the living room with the question.

Her sister appeared at the door almost immediately, apparently as eager to go as Evie herself felt. She had bought Mia some boots before leaving Oklahoma, and she was glad to see that her sister was wearing them. They would protect her feet far better than her athletic shoes if she got close to any horses.

Evie hoped that leaving the ranch wouldn't put them at risk for more danger, but Beau seemed to think it was safe enough, and his calm, steady manner was reassuring. Evie knew she couldn't stand to stay cooped up on the ranch indefinitely and staying on the property hadn't exactly helped so far. The patrols were supposed to be keeping an eye out for any suspicious activity and unfamiliar people, as well.

Harvey came loping up from the barn, and Beau urged him into the truck as they all got into the cab. It reminded Evie once again of what a great guy Beau had proven to be. Harvey perched carefully in the back seat of the truck, sticking his nose to the glass of one window until Beau cracked it.

The bright coral and buttery yellow rays of the morning sun washed over the landscape as Beau pulled into the long, dirt driveway leading to what looked like an ordinary ranch. The morning's mist hadn't quite cleared, and a light cloud of steam wafted up from a nearby pond as they passed. The sun was coming up a little later and settling below the horizon a little earlier with each passing day. Autumn was well on its way. The slight crispness that blew in with the breeze was just a hint of things to come, and Evie looked forward to it.

A slender woman of medium height met them in the driveway as they got out of the vehicle, her warm smile making Evie feel comfortable in her presence. She extended her hand, and Evie accepted it with a smile of her own. Harvey waited at the truck, settling into the open bed at Beau's command as if he had been following the man's directives all his life.

"You must be Evie. I'm Whitney Sharum.

So glad to meet you." Her soft voice was just as welcoming as her smile.

"Nice to meet you, Whitney. This is my sister, Mia." Evie gestured toward her sister, who was trailing her closely. Her expression betrayed a bit of nervousness if Evie wasn't mistaken as she looked around the horse rescue center.

"Hello, Mia. I'm glad you came." After smiling at the younger girl, Whitney turned to Beau. "Thanks for thinking of us. I hope we have what you're looking for. It's so hard to find homes for some of these horses."

"I know it is, but I think they might be a perfect fit for Evie. She will probably have riders of all experience levels in her program. Some may never have been on a horse before." Beau glanced her way, making Evie's heartbeat accelerate.

"Some of the horses we have still need a purpose, despite their age. There's a lot of life left in some of them. But when they get too old to compete or breed, many people need to replace them and just don't have the room for the older horses on their feed bill." Whitney spoke as she led the way down to a paddock where many horses grazed. "It's a sad fact of life for many of these animals."

Evie's heart wrenched for the horses. She

had always been an animal lover and hated to see any of them cast away. "Hopefully, I can give some of them just the home and the purpose they need."

As they approached the corral, some of the horses raised their heads in curiosity, and some even meandered toward the fence nearest them. The horses all appeared to be in good condition, mostly due to the care they received here at the rescue center, she was sure. Evie looked over the horses that stood closest to the fence, liking what she saw so far.

Mia, however, went straight to a bay horse who stood alone on the far side of the pen. He was tall, lanky and a little bit on the thin side, but when Mia carefully approached the fence where he stood, he lowered his head and his eyes softened. She spoke gently to him, and Evie stood watching in amazement as the horse stepped toward the hand Mia stretched toward him.

"I want this one," Mia said quietly.

Beau leaned toward Evie. "You're in trouble there. She has a good heart and a good eye. With a little love and some extra oats, that will make her a fine horse."

Evie glanced at him questioningly. "How can you tell?"

"Partly his conformation. He's well-bred.

He's got kind eyes and a good demeanor. But also, I recognize the brand. He was rescued from the Gable Ranch after the owner died. They bred fine horses, but there was no one to take over for the previous owner. A nephew out in California inherited the ranch, but he didn't want the horses. They were a little neglected until someone finally contacted Whitney that he wanted them gone. He didn't even bother to try to sell them."

"What a sad story." Evie's eyes clouded as she looked at Whitney.

The woman shrugged, but it was more of a gesture of uncertainty. "It's what we do. I try not to think about it."

The bay horse that had approached the fence stood with his eyes closed while Mia stroked his head.

"Beau is right, though. That's a good horse. I would have taken him for one of my own if I had the barn space." Whitney gave a nod. "I do think he has bonded with your sister, though."

Evie had to agree with her. The pair seemed to be communicating silently, and Evie was glad to see it. Mia needed that. And it was exactly what she hoped to achieve with her business, people easing their own hurts through creating bonds with the horses.

Whitney led Beau and Evie into the paddock then and walked them through the horses, telling them what she knew about each one. "These are the gentlest ones that I have. I don't think you could go wrong with any of these. Some are getting on up in years, but they're safe. They're healthy as well, despite their years. I've ridden all of them to be sure. My four-year-old niece even rode with me on a couple of them, and my daughter has helped me with grooming them. She's only nine years old."

Mia's attention was piqued at this statement. She was nine and a half herself, so she probably wondered about the girl.

Evie walked through the horses, realizing this might have been a bad idea. Not because she wasn't finding what she needed, but because she found she wanted to take them all home. She just didn't have that kind of money to get started with.

"How will I ever decide?" Evie lamented. "They all seem so sweet."

There were seven horses in the corral, and she had only figured on keeping four or five to start off. She couldn't really justify taking all seven right now. But she could see the sorrow on Mia's face as she spoke the words.

"Why don't we try them all out?" Beau said softly. "If you don't need them all, maybe I can find a job for a few of them. I always need a backup horse on the ranch, and some might be needed at your place later. If not, we can always find a home for them then."

Mia's countenance brightened and Evie breathed a relieved sigh. "I do think we should probably ride and work with them all to get to know them and see which ones will be the best fit for therapeutic purposes."

Whitney, too, looked happy to hear this news. "That's great! Do we need to keep them here for a few days until you can get them situated?"

Beau shook his head. "I can have the guys come pick them up this afternoon."

"Perfect. I just have some paperwork we need to take care of. Do you mind following me back to the office?" Whitney asked.

They agreed, and she led them to a large sheet-metal building where they followed her inside. When they reached the office, a young girl who looked to be about Mia's age hopped out of the chair behind the desk with an impish grin.

"This is my daughter, Norah. She came to help me out at work today. Norah, this is Mia. Can you show her around while we take care of some things?"

Norah nodded and skipped over to say hello to Mia. They exchanged tentative smiles.

"Now, no petting the kittens." Whitney shooed the girls out the door to a chorus of giggles.

"I hope Harvey stays at the truck. I'm not sure he would know not to chase the barn cats." Evie made a worried face at the door.

"He's a good dog. I doubt he'll cause them any problems." Beau's tone reassured her as they settled into the chairs Whitney offered to them.

"He'll be fine. Those cats are used to all kinds of commotion," Whitney agreed.

She produced papers for the horses she had registration for, though some of them were either grade horses with no breed registration, or the identifying papers for them had been lost somewhere along the way. Evie assured her it didn't matter. She didn't intend to show or breed any of the horses, which was the only real reason she might need them.

By the time they had finished up, Norah was leading Mia on a merry chase around the stable yard, and Mia was climbing fences and hopping off hay bales like she had grown up in the country.

"Mia, it's time to go."

Evie's directive was met with a groan from her sister.

"Do we have to? The kittens were asleep, and we were gonna go back to play with them." Mia's face was flushed, and she looked tousled from running around the stable yard with Norah. Evie was heartened to see her sister enjoying herself. She hoped Mia had made a friend she would see at school when she started next week.

"Yes, but maybe Norah can come over soon." Evie looked at Norah and then at Whitney. "If it's okay with her mom."

She didn't mention that it would have to be after she figured out this whole mess with Ruark and the stolen money, but when she caught Beau's cautionary look, she nodded to indicate that she had already thought of the situation.

"Oh, I'm sure we can get some playdates set up before too long." Whitney smiled. "I'm glad you two got along."

Mia followed Evie and Beau to the truck, but she was pouty well into their departure. Pulling Harvey into her lap only pacified her slightly.

They didn't get far down the road before Mia's eyes grew heavy. Evie envied her ability to sleep. All the things happening lately were taking a toll on them all, and Evie's own sleep habits had certainly suffered.

They reached a turnoff, and as they made the corner, they noticed a sheriff's patrol car pulled over beside the ditch. It was dented and looked deserted just sitting on the side of the road.

"That's strange." Beau pulled the truck to a stop right behind it.

"Where's the deputy? And the other car?" Evie felt a tingle of foreboding come over her. Harvey barked from the back seat.

"That's an excellent question. Call 911. I'm going to get us out of here in case it's a trick." Beau put the truck in reverse, but it was too late. A dark blue truck pulled up behind them, blocking them in. Beau slammed on the brakes to keep from backing into it.

"What now?" Evie was hitting Send on the call to the 911 dispatcher, but she knew even when she got through, it would take deputies a while to get to them.

Mia had become alert once more, and she spoke up from the back seat. "Someone's getting out of the truck."

Evie turned to look as the dispatcher answered. Both doors were opening on the truck.

"Two men in hoods and masks." Mia said it

quietly, but it pierced the quiet of the cab like a shout.

Beau glanced in his rearview mirror and shook his head. "Oh, no you aren't."

He hit the gas on the truck, still in reverse, and backed up as far as he could. When the bumpers connected, he shoved the shifter into drive, shooting around the patrol car and narrowly missing the back bumper. Thankfully he had stopped behind the patrol unit with some room to spare.

Evie watched as the men jumped back into the blue truck to follow. Mia squealed and clutched Harvey as their truck jerked forward. The other vehicle raced to catch up. Evie gripped the handle beside her head tightly, glancing between the front windshield and the back window. She reported what was going on to the dispatcher on the phone, who promised help was on the way before disconnecting.

"We aren't losing them," Evie warned. "What can we do?"

"I'm thinking. How long until help arrives?" Beau asked the question while trying to navigate a particularly sharp curve in the road.

"She didn't give a time estimate." Evie's voice shook as she answered. "Should I call back and ask?"

"No, it doesn't matter that much. I'll just

have to try to hold them off until help can get here." Beau shook his head, but before he could get ahead of the other truck coming out of the curve, they felt the impact of the blue truck's front bumper jarring them forward as it slammed into them from behind.

Mia was crying now, and Evie had a strong urge to join her. But she remained stoic, trying her best to soothe her little sister with soft words.

Beau was doing his best to keep the truck in the middle of the road ahead of the other one, but all the curves in the road made it impossible to go very fast. The ranches sat in valleys among the hilly terrain, and the roads between them twisted and turned like winding rivers.

Evie looked down the side of one particularly steep rise in the road and immediately wished she hadn't. The sheer drop was at least twenty or thirty feet to the ground. It made her stomach roll over to think about plunging off it.

The blue truck sped forward again, and Beau jerked left to avoid a direct impact from behind this time. When he did, however, another vehicle came around a curve toward them just ahead. He managed to react in time to avoid a collision, but his truck fishtailed and sent them into a skid. One wide tire dropped off the edge of the road where there was no shoulder and sent them spiraling off the incline on the side of the road.

Mia screamed and Evie gasped as the truck catapulted over the edge and rolled. Evie saw Beau's temple collide with the window near his head as the airbag deployed with brutal force, but she couldn't see anything more as the passenger-side airbag filled her own vision in the next instant. All the oxygen was knocked from her body, and she fought to gasp in a breath. She tried not to panic—she'd had the wind knocked out of herself before—but her body was crying out for air that she couldn't manage to take in.

The tightness in her chest eased at last, and she drew in a few slow breaths before pushing the airbag out of her face. The interior of the truck was eerily quiet, and Evie looked over at Beau. A knot was already rising on his temple and a trickle of blood oozed from it. She fought free of the seat belt and airbag and leaned over to check his pulse.

The steady rhythm at his wrist reassured her that he had only been knocked unconscious. Mia, too, appeared to be still, but perhaps only passed out from fear and shock.

Harvey whined then, bringing her attention back to her sister. The little dog seemed to be okay, thankfully, though he had to have taken quite a tumble around the vehicle. Perhaps Mia had held on to him, keeping him safe until she had passed out.

Evie was about to crawl into the back seat to check on her sister and Harvey when the door beside her wrenched open. Beefy hands clasped hold of her and dragged her from the cab of the truck.

Harvey barked, trying to come after the man, but he shoved the little dog back and slammed the truck door.

She began to fight to get loose, but her captor produced a gun before she could wrench herself free. She could hear Harvey still barking in the cab of the truck. He would surely wake up Beau and Mia soon.

The man pulled her away, a sense of urgency making him rougher as he growled at her from behind the mask. "You don't want anyone to get hurt, do you?"

He spoke in a gruff, deep voice as he waved the gun toward Mia and Beau, making his threat more imposing. When she didn't immediately respond, he gave her a little shake and she stopped fighting him.

"Okay. I'll go. Just don't hurt them." Evie allowed the man to prod her back up the incline and into the blue truck where the other man was getting back into the cab ahead of them.

Evie glanced back, only for a second, to where Beau and Mia were both still barely stirring, if at all, seemingly unaware of anything that was happening. Fear of a new kind clutched her middle. Harvey still barked frantically.

What if she never saw them again? What would become of Mia if anything happened to her?

Harvey's incessant barking was the first thing Beau became aware of when the fog cleared from his brain.

Mia howled in fear from the back seat. The truck sat at an odd angle, and every part of his body hurt, especially his head. He reached to push the airbag away and unfasten his seat belt.

"Shh, Mia, it's okay." He turned to soothe her. "Are you hurt?"

She calmed enough to answer him with a sniffle. Harvey, too, stopped barking for a moment, a whine letting him know all was not as it should be.

"I'm fine. It's Evie." Mia was gesturing wildly. Beau realized then that Evie's seat was empty.

Cold fear shot through him. "Where is she?"

"I saw a-a man with a gun dragging her away." Mia began to sob again. "And you wouldn't wake up."

Beau's stomach clenched as he rubbed the knot on his temple. His head throbbed unrelentingly. How long had he been unconscious? "When, Mia? How long ago?"

She was shaking her head. "I don't know. A few minutes?"

He knew she probably couldn't really give him an accurate measurement of time, but he had no way of knowing how great a head start they had gotten on him.

Beau tried to think, but Harvey's barks and whines kept piercing his head. "Did you see which way they went?"

Mia shrugged. "Toward the road."

Of course. That didn't help at all.

Before he could go after Evie, though, he needed to take care of Mia. He couldn't drag her along. He needed to make sure she was safe before he went anywhere.

The only option he really had was Whitney Sharum. He called 911 first and reported the incident, but then he called Whitney.

When she picked up, he got right to the point. "I need a huge favor."

He explained what had happened, and Whitney responded just as he had expected.

"Send me your location via text and I'll be right there to get Mia. I'm already on my way." He could hear the keys jingling in her hand.

Beau thanked Whitney and disconnected.

"Norah's mom is going to take me home?" Mia asked.

"Just until I can find your sister. You'll be safe with Whitney and Norah." Beau sent their location to Whitney's cell phone and then opened the truck door to get out. It stuck a bit, but it wasn't completely jammed.

Mia seemed to accept his idea, for she didn't say any more.

He stayed close to the truck, making his way around the outside of the vehicle, searching for anything that might help him find Evie. The mess of crushed grass and brush from the wreck was all he found, however, making him sigh in frustration. How would he figure out where they had taken her?

His head throbbed and concern for Evie made the seconds tick by far too slowly. He was jittery and anxious to go after her, but he knew it would take several minutes for Whitney to get here—precious minutes he might not have.

He didn't know what the men might do to

Evie if they found out she really didn't know anything about the money.

And not knowing where the men had taken her weighed on him as well.

Local deputies were likely doing all they could to help, but Beau decided to call Dean as well. Getting the sheriff directly involved made perfect sense to him, and since he wasn't sure how long it might be before Dean was made aware of the situation, he would make sure he knew right away.

When Beau told him what had happened, Dean didn't seem surprised at all. "I just heard from Whitney. I'm on my way also. Don't worry. We'll find her."

Beau wanted to latch on to Dean's confidence. Finding Evie before anything happened to her was everything. He stuck his head back into the truck to check on Mia then. He could still hear a few sniffles coming from the back seat. It pulled at his heartstrings. Mia had already lost so much in her young life. He would do everything he could to make sure she didn't lose her sister, too. *Lord, please help me find Evie and bring her back safe*, he prayed silently.

He helped Mia from the truck, and they made their way carefully up the embankment. Whitney and Dean would both be there soon.

Once they reached the road, Beau looked around for any evidence of the direction Evie's captors might have taken. He thought he could make out some faint tire marks, but he wasn't completely sure. It could be the product of a hopeful imagination. He would get Dean's opinion when he arrived.

For now, he had to keep his mind occupied so he wouldn't let his worry for Evie get to him. He needed to stay mentally sharp for the task ahead.

Mia remained quiet. Beau didn't try to change that. He thought she might be trying to process the situation, just as he was.

He began mentally constructing a plan for finding Evie. As far as he knew, she still had her cell phone on her. He hadn't found it anywhere around the scene of the wreck. They would start there. If that didn't work, they might have to split up and search in different directions. He at least had a good description of the truck to give authorities, if not a tag number.

Beau was hopeful that Evie's captors wouldn't harm her before he could find her since their main objective was to recover the money they thought she had in her possession.

The sound of an approaching vehicle brought his and Mia's attention to the road in the distance. He wasn't surprised to see Whitney's SUV appear first, but before she came to a stop, Dean's patrol vehicle came into view. He could see Whitney's anxious expression as she pulled up.

"Thanks for this, Whitney. I didn't know who to call. They don't know anyone around here." Beau spoke into the door as he helped Mia into Whitney's Tahoe beside Norah in the back seat.

"Not a bit of that, Beau Thorpe. You know I'm happy to help. I just wish I could do more." Whitney watched as Mia buckled her seat belt.

"This is exactly what we need." Beau gave the door a light tap with his right hand after closing it, speaking into the open window.

"We'll be at the house. Let me know something as soon as you can." Whitney looked down the embankment to where his truck lay smashed and dirty.

"Of course." He backed up as Whitney waved and blew a kiss toward her husband before driving away.

"Hop in." Dean had rolled down the window of his county SUV. "I'm assuming you have an idea of where to start looking?"

Beau jumped into the shotgun seat and nodded. "Do you think those are tire tracks? Coming back onto the road there?"

Dean squinted a moment. "Possibly. It's been dry lately, so no mud anywhere. But the dust seems to have a broken pattern there. We'll give it a shot."

He pulled the SUV onto the side road the other vehicle appeared to have taken. Beau described the truck the men had been driving, and Dean had a BOLO issued for the older model Chevy. He also requested a wrecker to retrieve Beau's truck as they sped along the road looking for any signs of Evie's captors.

The two-lane county roads were quiet. The twisting, curving asphalt hid so much of what lay ahead that Beau found himself straining his neck just to try to get a glimpse of anything farther than a couple dozen yards in front of them. Dean's own expression was one of concentrated seriousness.

"Do you think we could track her cell phone?" Beau knew Dean had probably already thought of that, but he brought it up anyway.

"I have someone on it. I should have told you." Dean nodded. "It isn't as quick and easy as they make it look on television, though."

"I don't imagine it would be very interesting to watch the actors sit around and wait for results." Beau grimaced. "I get that."

They drove on for a little while in silence.

When they reached a T in the road, however, they both looked at one another.

"Now what? Neither way is a direct route to anything special. Just more ranches and farmhouses." Beau looked right, then left, trying to think of any reason Evie's captors might want to take either direction.

"No, nothing special. Anything abandoned or secluded might appeal to these guys if they intended to harm her, but that doesn't seem to be their purpose. If they are only after the stolen money, I would think they would just try to take her to their boss." Dean's words echoed Beau's thoughts.

"Right, so if they came this way, they probably would have either turned around or just doubled back." Beau confirmed his agreement. He pulled up his GPS to take a closer look at the routes around them.

"I doubt they would have turned around in case of running into emergency responders at the scene of your accident. If we turn right, it goes out into nowhere, but if we go left, there are other roads that turn back toward the main highway, eventually back toward Cheyenne and an airport." Dean shrugged as he looked at the GPS maps Beau had pulled up.

"You think they might try to get her on a plane?" Beau asked.

"Unless the man after the money is also here." Dean frowned.

"Which brings us back full circle. If he's here in Wyoming, where would he be waiting for them? In town? At an abandoned house?" Beau shook his head. He was having trouble thinking like a criminal.

"We need that trace. Badly." Dean pushed a button on his vehicle's information screen and placed a call.

Beau gestured. "Go left. I'm going to trust my gut until we have more to go on."

Dean nodded and followed Beau's suggestion as the call rang through. A woman's voice answered. "Hi, Stephanie. Where are we on tracking that phone?"

"Let me check." The call clicked over to silence on the other end after Dean made a sound of agreement.

When she returned to the call a few seconds later, it was with some disappointing news. "Nothing yet. It may be that the phone is in a dead area. I'll call you back in five."

"Okay, thanks, Steph." Dean disconnected the call by tapping on the vehicle's screen once more.

"Do you think they've disabled it, or just lost signal?" Beau expected the worst.

"I'm sure they've taken the SIM card out

or smashed it by now. I'd hoped they would at least just discard it somewhere to give us a lead on the direction they took." Dean sped up as the road straightened out a little.

"And the truck? You'll be notified if anyone spots it?" Beau was trying so hard to think of something that his mind had gone blank.

"Yeah but check my phone messages just in case we missed something while I was talking to Stephanie." Dean handed the device to Beau after unlocking it.

"I don't see anything." Beau released a frustrated breath.

"Okay. Just help me look for any signs of them, then. They couldn't have gotten too far ahead of us." Dean drove on in silence after Beau agreed.

It was only a short time later when Beau began to think they might get a break at last. As they came up on another intersection, a vehicle sitting just to the side of the road came into view around the turn. It was a blue Chevy truck.

"What's going on here?" Dean asked. "Is that the truck?"

Beau reached for the door handle. "That's it."

"Wait," Dean cautioned. "It could be a trap."

He pulled his service weapon and Beau followed his lead. But as they got closer to the truck, something didn't feel right. He checked their surroundings, but there was nothing extraordinary. It was too quiet, though.

"Let's check inside." Dean motioned for Beau to be prepared as they opened the doors.

Beau grasped his own gun firmly with his left hand and, at Dean's nod, tore open the doors.

But the cab of the truck was completely empty.

TEN

Desperate fear filled Evie as her captors drove on silently toward town.

There were three of them now. The men had stopped the truck with no warning and pulled her out, confusing her with their actions. She could only decide they were trying to cover their trail by abandoning the truck that Beau could easily identify. When they had stuffed her into another vehicle, she had fought them, but her strength was nothing against three grown men, and it was only a couple of minutes before they had started off down the road with her trussed up in the back seat of an unobtrusive looking, newer-model white Honda Accord.

Beau would have no idea how to find her now.

They had taken her cell phone, smashed the SIM card and tossed what was left of the expensive device into the ditch shortly after taking her captive. Much to her surprise, they hadn't asked her anything about the money. She could only assume they were taking her to their boss.

Of the three men holding her hostage, only the tall slender one with dark hair and a suave manner seemed to have any authority. But she was still pretty positive he was working for someone else. The other two men seemed to be flunkies, or new recruits into the gang, or whatever. Evie knew nothing about how that sort of thing worked, and she hoped she didn't have to find out.

They drove into town, but only to get fuel, and then they took another two-lane highway off in the furthest direction from where they had left Beau and Mia. Evie worried for her little sister, wondering if she had been seriously injured in the crash, and what would become of her if anything happened to Evie. She also worried about Beau's injuries, knowing he had to at least have a mild concussion, but she had no idea what else. Would he even be able to come after her or report her missing? She had no way of knowing.

She knew her best bet would be to look for an opportunity to escape. Right now it seemed impossible, but surely the men would let their guard down eventually. She would be ready when they did. She wasn't about to give up yet. And until the opportunity came, she would keep sending up silent prayers.

One of the men, a young, short guy with long dirty-blond hair tied back in a bandana, sat in the back seat with her behind heavily tinted windows, and when he spoke to the men over the radio it startled her.

"Go ahead to the rendezvous spot. He said he would take it from there."

His voice was deep but had a bit of a twang to it. He wasn't from Wyoming, she didn't think.

"I hope that means we're getting paid." The guy driving interjected this remark. He had medium length, curly dark hair, and dark skin, but his eyes were a vivid green. He had an athletic build and stealthy manner. He had been the one to wave the gun at Evie, and she didn't like a single thing about him. He seemed cold and ruthless, and she couldn't wait to get out of his presence.

"You know we aren't getting paid until he gets the money." This from Mr. Suave, the urbane sophisticate who had met them with this car.

"I don't know why not. We did what he asked. We got her here. That's more than anyone else could do." The bandana kid said this. He sounded cocky to Evie.

She found herself wondering how many

hired thugs this villain had at his disposal. She knew of Rich White's reputation, but she didn't really know what that entailed. He was supposedly some sort of modern-day mobster, but that didn't mean a whole lot to Evie. She could only assume it meant a lot of people would do what he said.

"We aren't there yet. Don't get too cocky. In fact, you need to be a little more careful." Mr. Suave cut Bandana Boy a look.

"Me? You took a shortcut to pick us up instead of taking the route you were supposed to. That could have cost us. If someone saw you…" The kid shook his head, sending loose strands of hair dancing under his navy bandana.

"No one saw me. And besides, like I told you, I was running late. You would have been in more trouble if I hadn't made it here on time and that cowboy caught up with you before I arrived. He has too many friends around here." Mr. Suave was scanning the horizon as if afraid of Beau's far reach even now.

"He was out of it. Probably still wondering where he is." The driver spoke this time, and his words did nothing to reassure Evie. She hoped with everything in her he was wrong.

"You better hope so. You aren't getting any cash until this is done." This from Mr. Suave again. He seemed bored and annoyed with the whole situation. She had a feeling this wasn't exactly a first for him.

The men all fell silent again, and it wasn't long before they pulled into an overgrown lane that Evie would have missed if they hadn't turned onto it. The lane looked like it led to nowhere at first, and then slowly crawled down a little hill until the grass began to be overrun by trees of all sizes. After a while, she could see there was a tumbledown shack at the end of the rutted trail that looked like it had once been a gravel drive, and trees shrouded the whole property. The structure was old log slats that had holes between them large enough to let light pass through, and the whole thing seemed to be sagging in on itself as if it had given up the fight to stay upright. Nature seemed to be reclaiming what was hers all around it as grass and saplings grew up into every available crevice and nook. Nothing but field mice and opossums could have possibly inhabited the house in decades.

"He's not here yet." The driver spoke the obvious into the silence.

"He will be. Just give it a few minutes." Mr. Suave lowered the sun visor to check his hair in the mirror. Evie found it oddly amusing. Was he so concerned with what his boss thought? Or just vain in general?

She didn't have much time to ponder the thought, as a sleek black Mercedes with blacked-out windows crept down the drive. It was elegant, clean…and foreboding.

The men got out and two of them dragged her from the car, shoving her toward the Mercedes before it even came to a complete stop. It wasn't surprising to her that Mr. Suave let the other two do the dirty work, so to speak, as he approached the Mercedes, hands in the pockets of his tailored slacks, and spoke to the man who got out.

Evie was stunned. She sucked in a breath that almost choked her because of the gag in her mouth, but she couldn't hold it back.

She knew this man. She had seen him on more than one occasion. Ruark had never introduced her, simply explained later that he was a friend. But he had treated the man almost like a brother.

He had been around a great deal when they were dating, but never for long, almost as if he didn't want to be around her. She had thought him rude, but not a criminal.

This man was the infamous Rich White?

"I have some bad news."

Dean had pulled over at a convenience store after driving around in what felt like circles for at least a half hour. He had gone in for something to drink and to call the state investigation bureau. He had taken down the tag number and vehicle description to see if they could check them against owner records, though they suspected the vehicle was stolen.

Beau wasn't surprised by Dean's statement when he got back into the vehicle, though. It seemed they had gotten nothing *but* bad news. "Just hit me with it."

"The vehicle wasn't reported stolen." Dean paused.

"How is that bad news?" Beau knew more was coming.

"Because it was still likely stolen. The registered owner is recently deceased." Dean grimaced. "The man was murdered. No family members came forward to claim any of his belongings. Either the man had no one, or the family was involved."

"Are you checking into the family?" Beau latched on to this as a possible lead.

"Of course. But it could take time — something we don't really have much of." Dean gave him a sympathetic look.

"Then let's get to the nearest private airport. If Rich White is trying to recover his money, he might be trying to get her back to where it was stolen. If her ex-boyfriend stashed the money, it wouldn't be here in Wyoming. He will want to get her closer to his cash." Beau was sick of these games. He had to find Evie and get her back safely.

Dean didn't reply, just began driving to the private airstrip between Corduroy and Cheyenne. It wasn't a terribly short drive, but they had tried almost every other option. Abandoned farms were still deserted. No strange events had been reported around town. No links had been found among Rich White or Ruark Beaty and any of the locals. It seemed they were just chasing their tails.

Lord, give us some solid guidance, please. Beau sent up the silent prayer. He had learned when he was in the rangers to wait and trust. Sometimes it seemed like nothing was happening, but God was working. Something would shake loose. He trusted that it would.

A call came through with some good news at last. Dean had it on speaker when a detective in his county office named Boone Seawright gave him the news. "We have a connection. It's vague, but still a connection. The owner of the blue truck, Steven Wilcox, was in contact with a man in the Tulsa or Oklahoma City area. The cell phone number is registered to one Joseph Morton. It seems Morton has some ties to Rich White."

"Can you track Morton now?" Dean asked.

"Already did. He just happens to be in the area. I'm sending you his most recent location now." Detective Seawright spoke even as Dean's phone announced a text. The sheriff pulled to the side of the road and opened it.

"Perfect. Thanks Boone." Dean disconnected and plugged the location into his GPS.

As soon as he had it, he sped in that direction. "I think we were in this area earlier. Could we really have missed something?"

Beau frowned. "Maybe we missed Morton. Cross your fingers that maybe he's still close by."

Dean drove as fast as the curvy road would allow. The GPS eventually led them to a partially hidden driveway not far from where they were. "Oh, man. I forgot all about this place. It's easy to forget. I'm sorry, Beau."

"You couldn't be expected to remember every shady location in the county." Beau shook his head. "What is this place?"

"It was a homestead a hundred years ago, I think. Or somewhere close to that. If I'm not mistaken, the Haverty family had ties to it in some way. But it's long since been abandoned, decades ago, at least, and everything has grown up around it. I'm surprised the place still has a driveway," Dean said.

"It isn't much of one." Beau leaned forward.

"What are the odds he's still around somewhere?" Dean spoke his thoughts aloud.

In just that moment, a white Honda with two passengers appeared in the shadowy drive and almost ran into them head-on. Beau grabbed the handle beside his head as Dean swerved. "I think we found him."

The car tore off down the drive, throwing dust up in its wake. Dean whipped his SUV around the best he could in the tangle of bushes and vines overtaking the place and followed, turning on his lights and siren. They barely made it back to the main road in time to see what direction the car had taken. Dean followed it to the left, but the vehicle took the curves faster than his top-heavy SUV would allow, and the car soon gained a good lead.

Dean called in for backup and they followed the best they could, but it was going to take a roadblock or some other means to stop them. He radioed in to that effect. The driver of the car wasn't deterred in the least by Dean's flashing lights.

Almost fifteen minutes later the car came sliding to a sideways halt in the middle of the road when it encountered the roadblock Dean had requested.

To Beau's great shock, the men simply

stepped out of the car and put their hands in the air. He ran for the car and opened the door to the back seat.

Nothing.

Sucking in a breath, he moved to the trunk.

Empty.

They were too late. Evie was gone.

ELEVEN

Evie wriggled against her bonds until the movie-star handsome man driving the Mercedes finally glared at her. "It won't do you any good. Stop trying to get loose."

She glared back at him. He might think his good looks and charm would work on her since she was a female, but she was fully aware of what sort of evil could hide beneath an attractive surface. He was taking her back to Oklahoma City. He thought she had the money in her account. He had said as much, and though she had shaken her head at his ridiculous claims, he was convinced it was so. He wouldn't give up until he got her there to prove it.

She felt the raw places at the corners of her mouth beginning to sting where the gag was cutting them open. Her bonds were tight on her wrists and ankles as well, but they weren't unbearable just yet.

Her panic escalated when she saw that they were pulling into a private airstrip. How would Beau ever find her if this man put her on a plane and flew her back to Oklahoma? And what about Mia? She had only Evie, and she didn't know anyone here. Beau and the Sharums were the closest thing she had to friends, and they had just met. Evie had no way of knowing if they would see to it that Mia was taken care of. She thought they would, but it was a big thing to pin one's hopes on.

Besides, she wanted to be the one taking care of her sister. She wanted to be there for Mia and watch her grow up.

The private airstrip was quiet, and Evie knew there wasn't much she could do to get free. She fought against White when he pulled her from the car, but she couldn't really run with her ankles bound, so she couldn't get free for more than a few seconds at a time.

Tears filled her eyes as he dragged her to the plane and secured her inside. She looked toward the entrance to the airstrip, but it remained empty. No one was going to come for her in time. What could she do?

As the plane took off, she let the tears flow. She prayed fervently that she could survive this and get back to Mia safely.

Beau's handsome face also filled her thoughts.

She hadn't been interested in a relationship, but he had shown her kindness like she had never known from a man. She couldn't help thinking about what might have been.

She turned away from the window, but as she did, she thought she saw a county sheriff's SUV pulling into the airport. Was she right?

But when she looked back, all she could see was a sky full of clouds.

Beau's heart sank as the plane lifted off the ground.

It hadn't taken long to get the facts out of the men in the Honda, with the threat of going to jail hanging over their heads, especially since they were so smug that their boss had gotten away with Evie. Dean had assured them their cooperation was the only thing keeping them from being arrested. But Beau's frustration skyrocketed. Though they had jumped in the SUV and sped to the private airstrip, they had been just seconds too late.

"Come on," Dean commanded.

"What?" Beau was flustered. He could think of no way they could follow right now. He wasn't even sure where the plane was headed.

"I said come on, Mr. Army Ranger. You aren't giving up that easily, are you?" Dean broke into a sprint. Beau had no choice but to follow.

The sheriff led him to a hangar where a plane sat shrouded in dust. "It looks rough, but I'm sure it still flies the same. I know where the county keeps a fresh supply of fuel, since we were given permission to use it in case of emergencies. Just never had the chance before now."

Beau was shaking his head. "Oh, no. I gave up flying a long time ago. I don't even know if I can still fly a plane. Don't you have someone else we could call?"

"Do you want to waste that kind of time?"

Dean knew that back in his early days as a ranger, Beau had shown promise as a pilot. He also knew that a tragic accident had left him scarred and uncertain about flying. He still battled the nightmares to this day. The doctor had diagnosed him with PTSD and Beau had moved on, but he had never gotten back into the cockpit of a plane. He didn't mind jumping from them with his Airborne unit, but he just couldn't bring himself to pilot another C-17. There was too much at risk.

Dean brought him back to the present with his next comment. "Do you want to take the risk of waiting on a commercial flight or another pilot? We could be there in a fraction of the time."

"Whose plane is this, anyway?" Beau asked.

"Never mind that. You're wasting time. Are you going to fly it?" Dean was scrutinizing him.

Beau felt a hot flush come over his body. His adrenaline spiked at the thought. A rush of memories assaulted him from out of nowhere. He shook his head and pushed them away. He could do this. She *needed* him to do this. It might mean the difference between life and death for Evie.

He nodded at Dean and his friend gave him a huge grin. He couldn't believe he was agreeing to this. He felt sick.

Before he could process what was happening, he was in the cockpit of the plane, an older Cessna, and all the controls were staring him in the face. Flashes of memory flared in and out of his thoughts. He did his best to squash them, but they were relentless.

Beau took a deep breath as he vaguely registered Dean talking on the phone to Whitney as he began to check the mechanical gear. Everything seemed to be in good working order. The plane seemed safe enough.

He had thought that before.

He double-checked everything, and then he looked at Dean. Whitney was counting on him to keep her husband safe. Norah needed her father. The pressure was too much.

"Stay here. I can't take the risk of you not getting back to your wife and child. Let me go alone." Beau squeezed his eyes tightly shut.

"No. You can't do this alone. You need my help. I trust you." Dean said the words firmly and with conviction.

I trust you.

Beau wasn't asking for his trust. He knew very well he wasn't worthy of Dean's trust. What if he failed? He would never forgive himself.

Evie's lovely face swam into his mind. She had gotten to him, for sure. He couldn't fail her. He couldn't fail Mia. He had to do this, and soon. Dean wasn't budging.

Beau took a deep breath and let it out fast. "Fasten your seat belt."

"That's the Beau Thorpe I know." Dean smiled and did as Beau asked.

In minutes, they were in the air.

TWELVE

Somehow Evie had fallen asleep. She could only chalk it up to sheer mental exhaustion, but when she awoke, the plane was landing, and Rich White was on the phone with someone. His tone was not so charming at the moment.

He noticed her open eyelids about that time, and he growled into the receiver. "I'll call you back."

Evie watched as he leaned toward her. He pulled the gag from her mouth. She just stared. She had nothing to say to this monster.

"Here's the plan. We are going to the bank where you have my money stashed. You are going to withdraw every bit of it. I don't care what you put on the paperwork the bank is requesting. Tell them you are buying a mansion, a company, moving to Tahiti, I don't care. But I'll be with you the whole time. If you don't do exactly as I say, you won't see your little sister ever again, do you understand?"

Evie nodded. She wouldn't give him the satisfaction of showing any fear. He had brought her here, and if he really thought she could pull the money from her account, she would deal with the consequences when he realized it wasn't there.

She tried not to panic at the thought of what he might do when he realized she didn't have his money. One step at a time. Maybe she could somehow alert the bank staff to call the police for her.

"Don't get any ideas about alerting the police, either." He must have read her expression. She had tried so hard to keep it blank.

She blinked slowly and just nodded.

"What, nothing to say now? No arguments? No protests that you don't have my money?" He laughed, but it wasn't a jovial sound.

She didn't reply, just turned her head away.

That seemed to anger him. He backhanded her across the face. "It's rude to ignore someone when they're speaking to you."

Evie just wiped the trickle of blood from the corner of her already cracked lip. She half expected him to backhand her again when she didn't reply, but instead he began unfastening their seat belts.

He showed her a nasty looking Ruger and

stuck it in his waistband under his jacket. "You won't make me use this, right?"

She shook her head, afraid of what he might do this time if she didn't at least acknowledge his question.

"Good girl. Too bad you aren't a more honest person, Evie. We could have gotten along really well." He ran a manicured finger down her cheek and across her chin.

She barely contained her shudder.

They made a short drive from the unfamiliar airstrip to a bank, and rather than another Mercedes, her captor had a black Maserati SUV waiting this time. He did seem to like his luxury cars, she couldn't help thinking. He didn't unfasten her bonds completely until they pulled up outside the Liberty Union National Bank and Trust. He parked as far as he could get from the entrance of the bank. She realized no one would be suspicious. They would just think he was protecting his fancy car.

"What is the amount that you think I have? I need to know how much to request to withdraw. And how do you want it?" She had to ask. She wouldn't be able to once she was inside. It would arouse suspicion, and there was no telling what he would do.

"The amount Ruark took, of course. Cash."

He tilted his head at her, as if not sure if she was playing games or not.

"I don't know how much he took. Or how much he spent." She raised her chin as if daring him to argue.

He stared at her for a moment. "You really don't?"

She shook her head.

"I thought you were in on it the whole time." He took out a piece of paper from his wallet and wrote down a dollar amount.

Her eyes widened. He clucked his tongue. "Now, now. Wasn't good ole Ruark ever honest with you?"

She didn't know how to respond to that. Of course he hadn't been.

They entered the bank, and as soon as it was their turn, Evie requested the withdrawal amount from the teller. Her eyes widened as well, and she responded that she would have to get her manager. The teller first asked for her account number. She pulled it up on her phone where the number had been saved to her notes. She didn't have an app for the bank account. She hadn't withdrawn money from it in several months.

Evie's nerves were already frazzled, and this made her heart speed into overdrive. She looked at Rich White, not sure what he would do. He just nodded calmly. Apparently this was common practice. She wouldn't know, of course.

She waited in miserable fear. What was he going to do when they announced she didn't have that kind of money in her account? Would he drag her outside before attacking her? Or would he cause a scene right here?

She didn't have to wait long.

A few minutes passed and the manager appeared and requested her identification. Her heart hammered. "I'm afraid I don't have it on me."

"Just one moment then, please. You have your account number?" The bank manager looked at Evie before turning to the teller, who still waited behind him.

The teller handed over Evie's number and the bank manager disappeared. Anxiousness filled her. Was he going to call the authorities? He must know she didn't have the money, even if she did have her ID.

The bank manager returned with a sheaf of papers. "Sign these acknowledging that the bank withdrawals this money in your name in good faith. Your picture is on file. If the signature is adequate, you can make the withdrawal."

She did so, and he looked them over when she handed the papers back.

He then nodded at the teller, signed the papers and requested assistance from security at the vault.

Evie's mouth hung open. The money was there? In her account all along? How had he done this, and she had never even known?

True, she watched her checking account diligently, but rarely checked her savings. Still, this was beyond her comprehension.

Once the transaction was complete, the teller picked up the phone and asked for a security guard. When the uniformed man appeared, he escorted them out. They thanked him when they reached White's car, Evie's head still reeling.

"You really didn't know, did you?" Rich White was staring at her, his expression conveying his pity.

"What now?" She choked out the question. "Are you going to kill me?"

He laughed. "Nah. The police will be coming for you soon enough. I made sure to plant enough evidence to get you convicted of Ruark's murder. Now that we've withdrawn the money, no doubt they will come for you soon. The bank will have to report such a large withdrawal amount, and you've already been flagged by investigators. Didn't the detectives interview you?"

He seemed to know everything. Evie had no defense against what he said. She was going to look as guilty as could be, and she had no idea how this had even happened. And she had no one to help her.

Rich White gave her a smirk, got into the SUV and drove away. Evie collapsed onto the sidewalk. She had no idea what to do now. She had no cell phone, no money—ironic considering there had just been millions in her account—and no one to turn to. If she called Beau now, he would know she was a liar and a fraud.

He would never believe she hadn't known.

She began to walk. She would go to the police station. They might never believe her, but she had to try.

Beau landed the plane with a sigh of relief. He couldn't believe they had made it safely. But that was just the beginning. How did they find Evie now?

Shortly after they had exited the plane, Dean motioned him over to where he stood talking to a man in a custodial uniform. "A black Maserati SUV. Oklahoma tag that says, 'Boo-G' on it. Corny if you ask me."

Beau had to agree with Dean's assessment.

Dean had called ahead to local authorities, and a local police officer was waiting for them.

They soon tracked the SUV to a bank in midtown.

"There." Beau spotted it leaving the bank's parking lot.

They followed in the city police cruiser, weaving in and out of traffic, and finally succeeded in pulling the vehicle over. Rich White got out of the Maserati, but no one else.

"Maybe she's inside." Dean said this as he exchanged a look with Beau.

However, the SUV was empty.

"Where is she?" Beau demanded. "Where's Evie?"

White simply shrugged. "I don't know what you're talking about."

"I know she was with you. We have witnesses." Beau's face felt hot with anger. If this man had hurt Evie, he didn't know what he might do.

White turned to the police officer. "Do you have any reason to detain me? I know my rights."

The cop looked at Beau apologetically and shook his head.

As Rich White got back into the car, he made sure Beau saw the briefcase. He was trying to send Beau a message. He just wasn't sure what that message was.

Beau wanted to scream with frustration. He

stood there helplessly watching White drive away until he spotted something that made his heart nearly stop beating.

There was a woman walking beside the road that looked just like Evie. No way.

"Stop!" He blurted out the word. "Turn around."

The police officer did as he asked, and Beau couldn't believe it when they pulled to a stop. He was out of the vehicle in an instant and stepping toward her.

"Evie?"

As soon as she saw him, she melted into a heap. "How did you find me?"

He didn't have time to answer. Sirens sounded behind them at that moment. They came screeching to a halt, and Beau stepped back in shock.

A cop stepped out of one of the police cruisers. "Ma'am, please put your hands in the air."

"What's going on?" Dean demanded.

A detective in plain clothes stepped closer and put handcuffs on Evie. "This woman is under arrest for the murder of Ruark Beaty."

"This is a misunderstanding. She didn't kill him. Did you, Evie?" Beau hated the shred of doubt he heard in his voice.

"Of course not." Evie looked completely panic-stricken. "But Rich White made it look like I did. I don't know if I can prove my innocence."

Beau felt the same way. "What evidence do you have? How can you arrest her?"

The detective simply stared at him.

"He doesn't have to tell you anything, Beau. You know that. We just need to get her a lawyer." Dean had followed Beau from the vehicle and was trying to reason with him now. "We'll have to go about it another way."

"We can't let them take her into custody. What can we do?" Beau started toward Evie, but Dean grabbed his arm.

"Not now. You're just going to get yourself into trouble." Dean spoke quietly in his ear.

The officer was reading Evie her rights, and the look of sheer horror on her face made his heart seize in his chest. The cop put her into the car, and he couldn't stand it anymore. He looked away.

"Come on." Dean led him back to the police cruiser they had arrived in. "We'll go to the station and see what we can do about working this all out."

But when they arrived, the detective had taken her to an interrogation room.

"I'll see what I can find out." Dean indicated his uniform and badge, making it clear to Beau that he would be more likely to get answers.

Beau paced while he waited. There was no telling what kind of strings a man like Rich White could pull. He had no doubt White had framed Evie. He just had no idea what to do about it. He called his brother and left a voice mail asking him to return his call. Caldwell had completed law school and practiced criminal law for a few years before deciding he wanted something different out of life. He hadn't lived near the rest of the Thorpe brothers for years, but Beau hoped with fervency that he would help his brother out now.

He could do nothing but wait, and when Dean returned, he didn't like what his friend had to say either. "She had the money in her account."

"How? I know she didn't put it there. It's too obvious. No one would put it in their bank account if they had killed the person who was rumored to have it." Beau was shaking his head at the absurdity of the whole thing.

"I agree. But detectives aren't looking at it that way. They think they have an easy case." Dean sighed. "I'm no detective, but if it's too easy, it probably isn't so."

"Right. I called Caldwell. Maybe I should call Avery as well. If nothing else, maybe I can prove who actually did it." Beau looked over Dean's shoulder at nothing at all, thinking.

Avery was a private detective in Corduroy, recently married. But he had once worked as a detective for the state. He knew a thing or two about investigating.

"I'll do everything I can to help." Dean clapped him on the shoulder. "She'll get a trial."

Beau called Avery and told him the details.

Avery gave a low whistle. "So much we need to catch up on, bro."

"I agree. But right now, what can you tell me about finding the real killer." Beau didn't have time to mince words.

"I'd start with finding out who put the money in her account."

THIRTEEN

Evie endured questioning until she couldn't hold back the tears of frustration. She was terrified. She knew Beau was out there in the precinct somewhere, which gave her some comfort, but she also didn't know why he was still there. She knew he had heard by now that the money had been found in her account. He must believe her guilty.

She was no match for a nasty villain like Rich White. She was going to prison. She knew she couldn't figure out a way out of this one. She had heard stories of innocent people being convicted of crimes they didn't commit, but it had never seemed more real.

No one had shown her the least amount of kindness. She felt like everyone she encountered saw "guilty" as soon as they looked at her.

When the detectives finally left her alone for a few minutes, she prayed harder than she ever had. She knew of no other way but to trust in God to get her through this.

A gruff looking Hispanic officer opened the door. "Your lawyer is here."

"My… I don't have a lawyer." Evie frowned.

"You do now." This came from somewhere behind the policeman.

A thin man of medium height with sandy hair and glasses pushed past the officer. The newcomer held out his hand toward Evie. "Foster Golding. I'm a former colleague of Caldwell Thorpe's, and you, my dear, are free to go. I'll escort you out."

Evie couldn't believe her ears. "I'm sorry?"

"We're out of here. I'll explain when we get downstairs." He smiled.

To her amazement, the cop allowed them to pass. Beyond the door, Beau waited. She collapsed against him before she could think of the repercussions. The jump in her heart rate reminded her immediately of why it was a bad idea.

Evie pulled back. "I can't believe you're still here. I know you must think the worst."

"We'll figure all that out later. Right now you have a little sister who is waiting anxiously to hear from you." Beau laid a hand on the small of her back and they moved out of the precinct as a group, Dean and Foster Golding right behind them.

Once they were in Foster's car driving out of the parking lot, Evie couldn't hold back her questions any longer.

"How?" It was all she could muster.

"Technicalities, mainly. But also, they hadn't even checked your alibi for the time of the murder. Several witnesses were able to verify it. Someone was pretty certain you wouldn't be able to get good representation. I was happy to prove them wrong." Foster smiled with satisfaction.

Beau spoke up then also. "I called my brother Caldwell and before he even returned my call, he called Foster. He says Foster is the best lawyer he's ever seen, and he just happens to practice in Oklahoma City."

Foster sat a little straighter behind the wheel. "He gave me some pretty good competition while he was practicing. I still can't understand why he stopped."

Beau looked thoughtful. "None of us can. It's a total mystery."

"In any case, he proved to be right. I have never seen anyone get a murder suspect released so quickly." Dean chuckled.

"So the next step is getting White arrested and convicted. You told the detectives that he admitted to you that he killed Ruark?" Foster asked.

"Yes. I don't have any proof, but he told me that he killed him and made it look like I did it. I still don't understand how the money was put into my account, though. Was it Ruark before he died? Or put there by someone in Rich White's organization? Surely there is some footage of whoever made the deposit. It should be time-stamped, right?"

"It should be. I'm going to check into it and we will figure it out," Foster spoke again.

They talked for a short while until Foster pulled up to his law office. "Just give me a few minutes, and I'll give you a ride back to the airport."

"What about your fees?" Evie asked. "Do you need information from me for the account?"

Foster smiled once more. "Consider this a favor to Caldwell. Let's just say I owed him one or two. If anything else arises, we'll work something out."

Evie tried to protest, but Foster simply shook his head.

While he was gone, Evie called her sister on Beau's phone. Mia's relief at hearing her sister's voice echoed in her voice. Evie couldn't wait to see her sister and give her a huge hug.

Evie disconnected the call after a few minutes and turned to Beau. "So how do we get back to Wyoming? I'm not sure the authorities will just excuse my absence even though I was kidnapped. It isn't exactly a short drive, and I'm not sure how you guys got here."

Beau's face lost all color. "I flew us in a plane Dean's uncle owns."

She thought she had heard him wrong. "What? You flew the plane?"

Beau didn't look at her. He seemed a little nauseated, actually. "Yeah. I didn't have much choice. It was either that or waste time waiting for a pilot. We didn't have that kind of time. He told me later it was his uncle's plane."

His distracted manner spoke volumes.

He cleared his throat before speaking again. "Dean can make sure you're okay to go."

Dean nodded. "I told them when they were processing your release that you would remain under my protection. They know I wouldn't endanger my career by not getting you back here if they say so."

Evie thanked him but her mind returned to what Beau had just told her. She didn't know what to say or even what to think about him overcoming his past trauma to fly a plane. She sat there wondering if she looked as stunned as she felt. He hadn't flown a plane since the crash that had killed his friend Canaan. Yet he was willing to fly again to come and rescue her. What did that mean? Dare she hope it meant he was developing feelings for her?

She squashed the thought. She couldn't. She wouldn't. She knew the truth, no matter how drawn to his kind, tender nature she might be.

Neither of them was anywhere close to being ready for love.

Beau's relief at being back on solid ground in Wyoming was short-lived.

White must have gotten word that Evie was no longer a suspect in Ruark's murder. Now he wanted to cover his tracks.

Dean had left the airstrip minutes after the plane landed just before a barrage of shots began to rain down on the parking area outside the hangar. Beau had called for Payne to come pick them up, but the rancher had barely stuck a foot out the door to check on his hand's arrival when the shooting began.

He reacted quickly, urging Evie back inside. "Call Dean first. He can't have gotten far. Then dial 911."

He handed his phone to Evie and pulled his Glock. Staying low, he peered out to try to locate the source of the gunfire. It was too quiet around them. There were low, open fields on one side of the airstrip with a few remote manufacturing businesses beyond. On the other side, there were some trees where the hills began to rise again. That had to be where the shooter was hiding.

"There's no answer. Should I leave a voice mail? For Dean, I mean." Evie looked stricken.

He was wondering the same thing she probably was: *Is he okay?*

"Yes, and then get 911 on the phone ASAP. Let them know the sheriff isn't answering as well. Someone needs to check on him." Beau glanced over his shoulder for only a split second before focusing on the scene outside the hangar once more.

He could hear her speaking to the dispatcher in anxious tones behind him. He didn't focus on her words, though. He was coming up with a plan. When she disconnected, he would call Payne and see where he was. If he came in from the other direction, he might be able to sneak in behind the shooter before anyone knew he was there. In the meantime, he and Evie could slip out of the hangar on the far side and make their way around to safety among the trees and the hills. They would have to hurry to make it while Payne had White's people distracted.

She disconnected and he explained it to her.

Evie's eyes were wide, but she nodded. "So once we escape into the hills, what then?"

"Hopefully the sheriff's deputies will be here, and we can catch a ride back to the ranch. Let's take it one step at a time, though." Beau didn't want to say it, but he knew there were a number of things that could go wrong.

He took his phone from Evie and called Payne. He was close, but he promised to turn around and change his approach. When he was finally close, Beau led Evie out the far side of the hangar, and they crept quietly away until they reached an area where they would be visible from the other side. They broke into a sprint just as shots began again. He didn't take the time to check to see if it was Payne or them the guy was shooting at, he just kept Evie moving.

The trees were sparse, but they gave more cover than the open spaces, so he weaved in and out of them, trying to make sure Evie was keeping up. A shot finally glanced off the bark of a tree just ahead of them, and he urged her to move more quickly. More shots sounded around them.

She let out a sudden yelp.

"Beau!" She began to slow. "My leg hurts. Just a graze I think, but I'm hit. It feels like I'm bleeding."

He slowed long enough to glance back. Sure enough, blood seeped through her jeans just below her knee, and there was a ragged spot above the stain.

He doubled back for a moment. "Just relax. I'll put you on my back."

She nodded. He swooped under her and gathered her up. She felt like a child as he dashed over the remaining hillside, keeping them both low. He slowed only a bit as his legs churned higher up the hill. When he crested, however, they bounded down and into a low space.

A few more bullets kicked up dirt at the crest of the hill, but they couldn't reach them through the earth's swell. Beau gently lowered Evie to the dirt, careful to avoid any sharp rocks.

"Let's get a look at that wound." He gave her an apologetic glance before grasping the fabric of her jeans around the knee and ripping the hole wider.

It was a flesh wound, but deep enough that she might need stitches. "Just the soft tissue in your calf muscle. It's lucky it wasn't a little higher. I'm not sure your knee would have fared as well. But this is easily repaired."

He pulled off his overshirt and held it to the wound, trying to slow the flow of blood. Evie sucked in a breath at the touch, but otherwise didn't let on that it hurt too badly. Her face was a steely mask of determination. No doubt she was trying not to think about the pain.

"You think it'll need stitches?" She glanced at the blood soaking through his plaid shirt where he held it against her leg. He had just said it might, but she was hoping it wasn't as bad as he first thought.

"Most likely. But that's not too bad." Beau smiled at her.

The gunfire had stopped. They should hear sirens anytime, but there was still no sound at all echoing through the hills, save the occasional bird or insect. The day was warm for this late in the year, and he could feel the sweat soaking through his undershirt. There was only an occasional light breeze to temper the warm rays of the sun beaming down on them.

But even so, Beau was hyperaware of Evie's presence beside him.

Her breathing was quick, probably as much from the pain of her wound as the exertion before she was hit. He was trained in emergency medical techniques from the rangers, so he knew her wound wasn't life-threatening, but he hated not being able to do more for her. Her pretty face was pale, and he suspected she was also frightened.

"It will be okay. I promise we will get out of here soon." Beau tried to convey his sincerity through his gaze. When her vulnerable expression returned to him, however, he found a tender longing to comfort her in his arms flooding his being.

She startled him with her words. "Why did you fly the plane? I know how hard that must have been for you."

An ache hit him hard and fast in the middle of his chest. He didn't know if he was ready to talk about this. "I didn't really have a choice."

"You did. You could have waited." Her voice wasn't accusatory. Instead, it was full of wonder, like she couldn't quite reconcile what she thought to be true with the facts.

"I knew we didn't have time to waste. The benefits outweighed the risks. I couldn't let anything happen to someone I cared about."

Her face flushed at his words. At that moment he wanted more than ever to wrap her tenderly in his arms. To ease her discomfort. To make her feel safe. To calm her shivers from the shock.

Maybe even to see how her lips felt against his own.

He almost gave in.

He found himself leaning toward her when the sirens finally resounded through the air. He pulled back, looking down at her bleeding leg as reality swept through him. What was he doing?

This was not on the agenda.

FOURTEEN

Evie heard the sirens, but they seemed surreal. Until Beau pulled away.

He had been about to kiss her.

And honestly, she had wanted him to. She knew she shouldn't. She shouldn't have wanted him to or let him kiss her, but she had been about to lean toward him, too. That was more than consenting, that was participating. What did that say about her?

The shock must be getting to her. That was all she could figure out. The events of the past few days had her in a mental conundrum, and she wasn't thinking clearly.

"Wait here a moment, and I'll see what is going on. Hold pressure on this until I can get back." Beau indicated his shirt, and she took it, suddenly all too aware that his personal belonging was against her flesh.

The pain felt secondary to the tender feelings for him washing through her, and she needed to clear her head. She watched him creep to the top of the hill and crouch low to peer over it. He came back, gripping his phone.

"I think they have everything under control, but I'm going to try Dean again just to be sure." He watched her until she nodded.

His face hardened again as it went to voice mail once more. "Still no answer. I'm calling Whitney."

Dean's wife answered on the second ring, and Evie could hear her responses through the phone. She thought Whitney said she hadn't talked to Dean either. Anxiety for the sheriff grew within her.

"We'll find him. Don't worry." Beau's expression was grim as he disconnected with Whitney.

"He's missing?" Evie asked.

"They aren't sure. He hasn't been answering his phone for anyone, and Whitney said her brother is headed out to look for him." Beau gestured. "Let's go see what the deputies have."

They made their way over the hill slowly until they were sure it was safe. Then they approached the deputies.

Beau didn't waste any time with niceties. "Where's the sheriff?"

"We've lost contact with him." One of the

younger deputies spoke up. "A couple of the guys went looking for him. His SUV hasn't been spotted yet, though."

Evie's heart hurt. She had put Dean in danger now also. Whitney had Norah as well as Mia to worry about, which should have been her responsibility as well. "This is all my fault."

Beau shook his head. "We should have seen this coming. White went to a lot of trouble to see you framed for Beaty's murder, and he isn't going to let you pin it back on him so easily. What's odd is that he doesn't usually make such sloppy mistakes."

"He thought it would be easy to make the police believe I did it." Evie had a sudden thought. "I wonder if Ruark put the money he hadn't already spent in my account. That must be why he was trying so hard to revive our relationship over the last few months. He thought he could have access to the money again."

"We'll find out." First responders were pulling up. Beau motioned for her to follow him. "Let's get you some medical attention."

Beau left her in the care of a medic as he went to speak with the other deputies. She watched his broad-shouldered form stride off with an air of confidence. She had no doubt he would do everything he could to take care of her.

The paramedic cleaned her wound and bandaged it. She then declared Evie to be all patched up. She gave Evie a reassuring smile. "You were lucky."

"No stitches?" Evie asked.

The dark-haired medic shook her head. "It should heal fine without them. It wasn't as deep as it looked."

"Thank you." Evie breathed.

"You're also lucky to have Beau Thorpe looking out for you, ya know. He's been a friend of the family for years. He's a real hero." The medic cast a fond look in his direction. "All those Thorpe brothers are pretty heroic. You know, his little brother Avery recently married. It was a sad day for all the single girls in Corduroy."

The medic gave a girlish giggle.

"Beau has only told me a little about his brothers." Evie tilted her head at the paramedic.

"He's apparently the only one still single. Grayson works for White House security, Briggs runs a ranch raising American bison and Avery is now a private investigator. But they were all in the military or law enforcement at one time or another." The paramedic filled her in on what she knew. "Only Avery and Beau still live here, though. You haven't met Avery and his wife, Brynn?"

"Oh, it isn't—it isn't like that between us. We're just acquaintances, really. But what about Caldwell? You didn't mention him." Evie stammered out her denial, knowing the pretty paramedic was imagining a relationship budding between Beau and Evie. Heat filled her face.

The woman gave her a knowing look. "Oh, okay. Sorry. Well, Caldwell is a bit of a mystery to everyone. He cut all ties with this town and his family for a while, and then suddenly the family learned he was married. But they didn't come back here. He didn't invite anyone to the wedding. It was all very odd."

Evie remembered Beau saying something to that effect. "Oh, I see."

She didn't mention what else Beau had said about Caldwell. She didn't know this woman well enough to trust her confidence. Besides, it wasn't her story to tell.

"But they're practically legends around here. Just a family of heroes." The paramedic walked away just as Beau headed back in her direction.

"They've found Dean's patrol unit. He wasn't inside. They're scouring the area for him now." His expression said he was scrambling to hold on to hope.

"And you want to be helping." Evie could see it on his face.

"I can't leave you. That may be just what they want. Dean's well trained. He will be okay." Beau's jaw had hardened into a steely expression. This was soldier mode. He was fighting his emotions and trusting his gut.

"The best thing we can do right now is get you back to the ranch and come up with a plan and put it into motion tomorrow. Tonight you need to rest. No doubt Mia's going to be happy to see you, too." Beau turned to the medic, who was walking in their direction. "She's free to go?"

The paramedic nodded at Beau and then gave Evie a wink.

"What was that about?" Beau gave her a confused look.

"I'll explain later." Evie smiled a little to herself. She didn't really look forward to explaining that to him. But it still gave her a happy little tingle, even if she knew it shouldn't.

As they left, Beau turned in the opposite direction of the ranch. "We're going to get you another phone before we head home. It's not safe for you to be without one, and the stores will be closing soon."

"Okay, I appreciate that." Evie hadn't even thought about the phone. She told him who her cellular carrier was, and they found the closest store. It was about to close, but when Beau had explained that it was an emergency, the clerk had looked at them with sympathy and allowed them in.

A very short while later, Evie had the security of a phone on her person once again. She breathed a sigh of relief that they hadn't given her any trouble on replacing it, thanks to the insurance she had often considered canceling. She was very glad now that she hadn't.

Whitney brought Mia to Beau's ranch to meet them. She ran at Evie full force, almost knocking her off balance when they arrived.

"Whoa, hey, kid. I'm happy to see you, too." She gave a little chuckle. "Did you grow while I was gone?"

Mia groaned. "I'm already too tall. I'm so glad you're okay, you big mean sister. I thought I'd never see you again."

"Oh, you aren't getting rid of me that easily." Evie made a mean face at her, then laughed.

Mia growled back and giggled. Then she snuggled up against Evie where she was curled on the couch. "What about Harvey? He missed you, too. Can he come in?"

"I don't know—" Evie began.

"Of course." Beau stood and went to the door to find the little dog. "He's been your protector. Maybe we should've had him with us."

Harvey ran in and settled on Evie's lap within easy reach of Mia's scratching fingers and wagged his scruffy tail.

Evie took a deep breath, enjoying the moment. She wished this homey scene would last forever. She could certainly get used to it.

Unfortunately, there was still a murderer on her trail.

Beau took the call outside when Dean's number rang in.

"I just want you to know I'm safe. One of them hijacked my unit after I spotted them and went in pursuit. I'll get back as soon as I can, but I'm on foot and one of them is still trailing me. I'll outsmart them soon and meet you. I assume you're at home?"

"Yes. But, hey, Dean, be careful. They found your unit, so there are guys out looking for you. Not sure how far it was from where you are now, though. Are you sure there's nothing I can do?" Beau was still torn. He felt the need to help his friend, but he couldn't leave Evie alone.

"Just take care of Evie. They're trying to draw you out so they can get to her. I'll send my location while I have a signal. You can send a rescue crew if that makes you feel better." Dean disconnected.

Beau received his location two seconds later, which he forwarded to another contact with the sheriff's department. They would get a team together and go bring him back.

Evie had gone to lay down and Mia, too, was in her room preparing to go to sleep. Beau was doodling out his thoughts on paper, trying to work through a plan on how to catch White. Evie wouldn't be safe until he was in custody.

The problem was getting to White before he got to Evie.

He was still pondering what to do, so he opened his email inbox. He had an email from Foster Golding, with an attached video. It was Evie's bank with footage of a woman making a transaction. She looked to be about Evie's size and build. She was wearing a hat, so her face was mostly covered by the angle of the camera, but the hair seemed to be blond like Evie's as well. He wasn't sure from just the video, but he thought it was the footage of the deposit into Evie's account. He didn't like what he was seeing.

What if Evie truly had known more than she had told him?

It wasn't unlikely that White had set this

up to make it look like Evie had made the deposit herself. He could very easily have found someone who looked enough like her to go in and deposit the money. It wouldn't be difficult to get her account number, and most bank employees wouldn't have many qualms about depositing money for someone without being positive of their identity. Withdrawal was another story, but since she would have simply been putting money in the account, there wasn't much reason to question it.

He closed the video and went back to the email, reading what Golding wrote. It was, indeed, the footage time-stamped for the time of the deposit. Actually, one of them. Apparently the deposit had been broken down over several different days. He went on to say that the videos all showed the same woman. To avoid suspicion? To see if Evie noticed? Or was it simply a matter of paperwork that would be required?

He couldn't be sure.

Beau went back to the video. He watched it to the end, but in none of them could he see the woman's face. He refused to believe it was Evie.

He didn't waste time with email. He called Golding right away, leaving him on speaker.

When Foster answered, Beau got right to

business. "Do you really think that's Evie? You can't see her face."

"I hadn't thought of that." Foster went quiet. "Let me pull up the other footage and see if there's a shot where you can see her face."

"You thought she was guilty?" Beau asked, his voice a little accusatory.

"Not of murder. Just keeping secrets." He cleared his throat. "It wouldn't be the first time a client had withheld information from me."

"You don't know her at all, then." Beau said it before he realized what he had said. "That's ridiculous. I'm sorry. Of course you don't know her. But I can tell you that's totally out of character."

"I appreciate your confidence in her, really. But you're right, I don't know her at all. I'm looking for footage that shows the woman's face clearly. If I find it, I'll send it to you, and you can verify whether it's her or not." Foster Golding kept his tone professional. Until he made one last statement. "I know you have feelings for her. Just be careful. Women aren't always what they seem."

Beau remained silent for a moment. "I'm aware of that. But I'm pretty sure Evie's exactly what she seems."

He disconnected with a sigh, only to look up

and see Evie standing in the door. Her stance was defensive, yet somehow still vulnerable.

"What's going on?" She asked the question softly, and he wasn't sure how much she had overheard.

He knew there was no point in keeping any of this from her. "Foster Golding forwarded me the video footage from your bank."

He didn't say any more, just showed her the video.

She drew in a sharp breath. "It looks like me."

He nodded.

Her eyes clouded. "Wait. Did you guys think this *was* me?"

"I knew it wasn't. I'm not sure Golding was convinced. But I asked him to send more footage if he could find some with a better shot of the face." Beau explained about the multiple deposits and told her that he hoped they could find one that would show the woman's face more clearly.

Evie was just shaking her head. "This is so crazy. He really went to great lengths to frame me. Strange he got careless with my alibi."

"He probably didn't consider that you might have one." Beau was frowning at his laptop screen. But he agreed it was odd that someone like White would miss that. "Even professional criminals like White slip up sometimes."

"More likely he thought I'd have no defense. After all, I'm sure he thinks I'm a nobody without any connections." Evie's eyes were downcast despite the small laugh she let out. Did she agree with him? Even on a subconscious level?

"Can you walk with me to the barn? I need to check on a foal that hasn't been feeling too well. We can talk on the way." He motioned for her to come with him.

She made a sound of agreement and went along.

The horses she had acquired from Whitney and the rescue center raised their heads from the corral as they walked by. She hadn't even had a chance to ride any of them yet.

They moved through the barn in companionable silence until they reached the end stall where a mare and young foal waited. The mother greeted the humans with a warning nicker.

"It's okay, mama. I just want to see how your baby's doing." Beau slid the stall door open and approached in a slow, quiet manner before squatting next to the foal.

"He's on his feet. That's an improvement." Beau felt around on the foal doing a brief examination. "I think he's going to be just fine. He's just had a bit of a rough start."

Evie stayed back, uttering soft reassurances to the mare while she watched Beau with the foal. He finished and stood to go.

"I know you get tired of following me around, but I want to make sure you're safe." He gave the mare a pat on the shoulder as he moved past her out of the stall.

"Not this part. I love taking care of the horses." She smiled.

"Well, good, because we need to go to the office so I can record the foal's illness and medication in my records. Just in case anything comes up later."

By the time they reached his office, he had a mental list of questions for her. He turned on his computer, but his attention was on her.

"Evie, this may not be the best time, but tell me about your life before moving to Wyoming." Beau sat back in his desk chair. She didn't hesitate before settling into a plush wingback chair near the window. It was dark out, but she turned to gaze through the wide wooden slats of the blinds anyway.

"My mother's name was Annette. She worked in many different careers, but the main ones I recall are the department store makeup counter when I was growing up and then, later, she landed a job as an airline flight attendant. My father was gone a lot—he was an archaeologist but also worked as a volunteer on various types of emergencies from medical to fire and disaster relief. I guess you could say he was a bit of a humanitarian. As I told you before, he disappeared when I was twelve, assumed dead. My mother met Davidoff Terrano through a friend who worked at the same airline, a pilot who flew for him privately from time to time. My mother was very beautiful, and Davidoff fell for her quickly. They married within a year, and she stopped working and became pregnant with my sister." She paused, glancing around to see that Mia wasn't anywhere around.

"You lived with them?" Beau couldn't imagine that was a good situation for her.

"For a couple of years, yes. But Davidoff didn't really like having me around. He never cared for me much, maybe because I saw through his shallow nature right away. Then my mother fell ill with pneumonia when Mia was just two. Davidoff hired a nanny, and I went to live with my paternal grandparents until college. I rarely saw Mia until she was much older. Even now, you'll notice, there is much we don't know about each other." Evie gave him a sad look.

"I can tell you really love her, though." Beau

wanted her to keep talking. "Where did you go to college?"

"I managed to get a scholarship for Oklahoma State. I wanted to go to veterinary school, but I didn't get accepted. They have one of the top vet programs in the nation, and it's very competitive to get in. I tried for a couple of years, but I just didn't have the connections to help boost my application. I did end up with a decent degree in animal science, though, and worked for some large-scale farms and ranches in western Oklahoma until I saved up enough to come here to follow my dreams of opening an equine therapy center." She had a far-off, dreamy look in her eyes. He knew she had to have been disappointed not to get her veterinary medicine degree, but she had obviously found a calling well suited to her outside that field.

"When did Mia come to live with you?" Beau asked.

"Just before I moved here. I didn't have custody of her immediately since Davidoff hadn't made any provisions for her guardianship before he died. But there was really no one else to care for her. No one who truly wanted her, at least. I wanted to make sure I had a home for her, not just some run-down duplex on the rough side of town." She made a face, realizing what she said.

He grinned. “I understand what you mean. A place where she has some space of her own.”

She nodded. “And I know the house is run-down now, but I have plans to make it beautiful again as soon as possible.”

“Speaking of that, I had a couple of the hands go take a look at it.” He cleared his throat.

“That bad?” Evie sighed.

“The plumbing and electrical wiring are a mess. But we can fix most of it. I might have to hire a professional electrician to update it to modern needs, though. That house was built in the forties if I’m not mistaken.” He shuffled some papers on his desk.

“I appreciate it. But I don’t know if I can afford it now.” She looked out the window again.

Beau took a deep breath. “Evie, I know it’s difficult for you to accept help. And I understand that. But let me loan you the money. We can deduct a small amount from your pay for helping here at the ranch, and I can give Mia some responsibilities as well. It will be good for her.”

“My pay? But I thought we were just exchanging help?” Evie’s brows furrowed.

“We were, initially. But I have realized I have a lot more I need done around here than I first thought. Could you do it until I find more help?" He slid a piece of paper to her. It was several days ago when he had started jotting down some of the things he needed help with.

"Oh. You already have it written up?" Evie picked up the paper.

"I was just going to write down what I would like for you to do. Then it just kept growing and the idea came to me." Beau shrugged. "It's not a bad idea, is it?"

Evie lowered the paper enough to give him a look that said she was suspicious of his motives. But she finally gave a little smile. "Okay. I do need a bit of income to help me until I get everything up and running."

He grinned broadly and extended his hand. "Welcome to the Lazy T Ranch."

Her eyes narrowed. "Your ranch name is pretty generic."

Beau laughed. "It actually doesn't even have one. I was making that up."

She just shook her head. "Maybe you can add naming the Thorpe ranch to my list of duties. I'm sure I can do better than that."

He couldn't hold back his laugh.

FIFTEEN

Shortly after their conversation, Dean had called and told Beau he was safely at home and promised to come first thing in the morning to tell him all about it. Beau had reported back to Evie before preparing to turn in for the night.

Evie lay awake thinking for a long time after leaving Beau's home office. She was glad for his help, though she still didn't really like the idea of accepting it. She knew it was necessary, though, if she was going to provide for Mia, and thanks to her sister and Beau's insight, she could see that repairing and improving the house was more important than she had first imagined it to be.

The other thing on her mind, however, was the video footage of the woman at the bank. Something about it filled her with unease. Whatever mistakes Rich White might have made with her alibi, he made up for them by prying into her life in other areas. He tracked down her bank account number, found a woman who looked like her enough to be inconspicuous making the deposits, and provided enough evidence that the police had tried to arrest her for it. He knew where she had lived before, tracked her here to Wyoming and had gone to great lengths to kidnap her. It was an eerie feeling knowing someone like him had invaded her privacy to such an extent. It made it difficult to sleep.

When her phone lit up a little after midnight, curiosity prompted her to pick it up.

Shock and horror made her drop the device when she read the sender's name.

The phone company had been able to retrieve all her contacts when she had gotten the new phone. She had never taken the time to delete Ruark's number, mainly because she had wanted to know if he began harassing her again not to answer it but seeing his name when he had been reported dead made her go cold. What kind of sick game was this?

She picked the phone up off the floor about the time a knock sounded at her door. "Evie, is everything okay?"

Beau must have heard her phone hit the floor.

"I—I'm not sure. Give me a second." She scrambled over to get her robe and threw it over her pajamas before taking the phone to the door.

When she opened the door, Beau's concerned expression almost made her crumple. He was full of so much goodness. He had already shown her so much kindness, and for no reason at all.

"I heard a loud noise," he explained.

She nodded and held out the phone. "I was so shocked I dropped it. I'm sorry I woke you."

His eyes widened when he saw the name. "I'm not. We need to call Dean."

"Should I open it? See what it says?" Evie asked.

"I don't think it matters. Someone is messing with your head." Beau had carried his phone with him and was already pulling up Dean's contact information.

Evie opened it. The message almost made her drop the phone again.

Did you give him my money? I trusted you to keep it safe.

Beau was watching her face. "What could be that bad?"

She showed him the message, shaking and pale. "Who else would know? Is it White, just trying to mess with me? Did he take Ruark's phone before he killed him?"

Beau looked angry. "Who knows. We will let Dean unravel this one."

She set the phone down, not wanting the message staring her in the face. It dinged again.

We could have had it made.

Evie turned it off. It wasn't him. She knew it couldn't be him. She tried to focus on Beau's conversation with Dean but words like *stalking* and *harassment* kept echoing in her mind.

When he disconnected, he told her what Dean had said. "Dean's going to look into the number tomorrow. He thinks they might be able to trace it and find out where the signal is coming from and if so, maybe they can track the person down. If it's White, all that much better, because they can arrest him and end this."

Evie nodded, but it was a robotic response. No way was she going to be able to sleep now.

Beau must have seen it in her expression. "Let's go down to the kitchen and get you some tea or something to settle your nerves." Beau gestured down the hall toward the stairs.

Mia stuck her head out of her room next door. She rubbed her eyes. "I heard voices."

"It's okay, sweetheart. Everything is fine. Go back to sleep." Evie reassured her with a wave of her hand.

Mia looked at Beau, who nodded. She accepted this confirmation, ducking back inside and closing the door.

Beau produced some herbal tea from the cabinet and gestured for Evie to sit. She did so and watched him heat water and slip a tea bag into the mug. She still hadn't spoken when he slid it before her.

"You know it's probably just another ploy to get to you. Rich White is a little nervous now that they are still looking for Ruark's murderer," Beau told her.

"But why? What good will it do him to hurt me? It won't help him get away with it." Evie was shaking her head in confusion.

"Who knows? Maybe he thinks you will confess to the murder anyway? Or maybe he just wants revenge. Who knows with a man like White." Beau laid one large, suntanned hand over hers, and she felt the tender gesture all the way to her soul. "But I'm not going to let him get to you. You're safe here."

She felt the moisture gathering in her eyes. "How will I ever repay you for all of this?"

He stared at her for a long moment. "Why do you think that every kind gesture needs repayment, Evie? Has no one ever been kind to you just for the sake of doing what's right?"

Her heart squeezed in her chest. "Not often, no. Only family. And I never had much of that."

She hated that the admission made her sound pitiful. She didn't want his sympathy. She would rather he respect her as a strong person.

"It's time someone did. You have taken care of yourself for so long. I know you are a strong woman, independent and self-sufficient. But you are deserving of kindness." He squeezed her hand, and she smiled through her misty eyes.

"Thank you."

Dean brought news that turned everything upside down the next morning.

Beau was still in the barn feeding horses with Payne when he walked down the stable aisle. He turned and greeted the sheriff with a handshake.

"Glad to see you in one piece." Beau looked Dean up and down but didn't see any sign of injury from the previous day's adventure.

"Me, too. That was an experience I could have done without. Look, can we talk somewhere about Evie's message?" He looked around the barn where a couple more hands were milling around.

"Sure. You know my cowhands are trustworthy, but we can go back to the house to my office if you'd rather." Beau dusted the feed bits from his hands and led the way, calling out his intention to Payne as he went.

Once they were settled in the office, Dean took off his Stetson and sat back with a sigh. "The FBI is involved."

"What? With Ruark's murder?" Beau couldn't cover his surprise.

"Yeah, it seems they think this might be their chance to nail Rich White to the wall. They have been trying to get to him for years. They see this as their big chance." Dean ran a hand through his sandy-blond hair.

"And what does that have to do with the message Evie got last night?"

Dean looked away. "They have Ruark's phone. According to the investigator I spoke to this morning, they need Evie's cooperation to put White away, but they need to know she's trustworthy."

"They thought she might incriminate herself if she thought Ruark was still alive?" Beau wasn't sure he was following.

"I think so. Of course, it doesn't guarantee anything to them that she didn't, but they'll be coming to talk to her soon. The good news about that is, she'll be heavily protected," Dean explained.

"Hmm." Beau put a finger to his lips. "For her cooperation?"

"Yes. And she may be called on to testify." Dean pressed his lips together. He didn't have to tell Beau what that meant. She would be put in WITSEC if that was the case. He wouldn't see her for months, maybe years.

The thought terrified him.

"Is there no other way?"

Dean was shaking his head. "It isn't looking like it at the moment."

Beau stood and walked to the window. "Then we need to make sure we get this taken care of quickly."

"How do you propose we do that? They haven't found White. He hasn't been seen since he made Evie withdraw his cash from the bank." Dean was shaking his head.

"He seems to want Evie out of the way. He'll be coming for her if the men he sends continue to fail." Beau didn't want to think of what it meant for them to succeed. He would be doing everything in his power to make sure that didn't happen.

"We need to be ready." Dean gave a nod of confirmation that he was now following. "I'll speak to the FBI agent. If we move quickly, maybe we can set up a trap for White before he ever knows the Feds are involved."

By the time Dean left, he and Beau had come up with a solid plan. Beau felt confident they could pull it off, as long as they could keep Evie safe. Dean left it to Beau, however, to tell Evie what she needed to know. He wasn't exactly looking forward to it.

He found her with Mia on the back patio. It was a nice day, and they were playing cornhole with some boards that one of the hands had pulled out of the barn for them. Their laughter was a nice break from the tension they had all been under lately, and Beau was loath to disrupt that peace. He knew he couldn't put it off for long, though.

He watched until they finished their game, which he was pretty sure Evie let Mia win, and then he told Evie he needed to speak to her. Mia ran off to the barn to help Payne groom some horses, and they settled into the patio chairs. Beau sat forward, elbows on his knees, and faced Evie.

"There's something you need to know about the message you received on your phone. The one from Ruark's number." He paused only a moment to be sure he had her full attention before telling her all about the FBI's involvement and what would be happening next. Her eyes widened, and she listened silently, only nodding occasionally until he reached the end of his commentary.

"You think I'm going to end up in witness protection?" She sat with her hands pressed between her knees, looking nervous and uncertain.

"It seems likely. I want you to know, even though we will have to cut all ties, I want to resume contact as soon as you're free to do so. I'll do everything I can to care for your property and the horses you've adopted from Whitney. The good news for you, however, is that Mia will probably be put under protection as well because of her close ties to you. You'll most likely get to stay together." He could see the scenario fleshing out in her mind as the reality of her situation came fully to rest on her shoulders.

"Wow. This is major." She whispered the words. "My life is never going to be the same, is it?"

"Not for a pretty good while. I'm so sorry you're having to face this." He didn't know what else to say.

When she crumpled, he reached for her. The feel of her soft warmth in his arms almost made him fall to pieces right along with her. He held her and let the quiet cries come. She seemed so strong. He couldn't believe how well she had been holding it together. Even now, she cried quietly for a few minutes, then wiped her eyes and apologized.

"You have nothing to be sorry for. You've been so strong." He stared into her eyes for a moment before she broke eye contact.

She shook her head as she looked away. "I haven't been. Not really. I'm just trying not to show it for Mia's sake."

He clasped her hand. "Well, you've done a terrific job of keeping calm."

She looked at him then. "Thank you. For everything."

He nodded. "I would do it again a million times over for you."

SIXTEEN

Evie couldn't hold her emotions in any longer. She was falling for Beau Thorpe. She wanted nothing more than to stay there in his strong, gentle embrace forever.

The thought of having to go into WITSEC was terrifying. She had heard stories of people who had gone into the witness protection program and had never come out. Their lives had changed completely. They had been forced to sever all contact with those they loved. The trials could drag on for years and normal life might never resume.

She might not ever see Beau again.

Her chest seized in protest at all the emotions swirling inside of her. She felt like her dreams, so close just a few moments ago, were all slipping away from her forever. How would she ever get on with her life?

Resentment toward Ruark filled her. For just a moment, she let the anger simmer inside her before pushing it away. It wouldn't do any good. Instead, she began to pray silently that the Lord would make this right. She knew there was a greater power at work in all of this, so she would choose to trust.

But it was going to take some work.

"Can you tell me what the plan is?" Evie asked.

Beau stared off toward the corrals in the distance. "Not all of it, really. And Dean has some things to work out with the FBI. But mostly it just involves waiting for White himself to make a move. If we have help from the FBI, it should give us the manpower to keep eyes on you at all times. Then when he does make a move, we'll be one step ahead of him."

Evie nodded. She didn't really need to know the finer details. She was as sure as Beau was that Rich White would eventually come after her himself. His manner when he had kidnapped her spoke of a man with an arrogant nature, who took matters into his own hands when things didn't go as he wanted them to. After all, hadn't he said he had killed Ruark himself? There were some things he wanted to deal with firsthand, it seemed. If she continued to escape his traps, she felt sure she would be one of those things.

"I think it best," Beau said slowly, "that Mia

stays with Whitney and Norah for a few days. They have a great security system and most likely just having Mia out of harm's way will make you feel better. If you are okay with that? Dean already mentioned it."

Evie thought for only a few seconds. It was her this evil man was after, not Mia, so separating from her sister until this was done only made sense. "Yes. I think you're right. She'll enjoy getting to know Norah better, and she can ride the bus with Norah when she starts school. It will ease her anxiety somewhat about starting school in a new place."

"I think Whitney usually takes Norah to school every morning and picks her up. That might be even better." Beau's tone was reassuring.

"Yes, she'll like that." Evie knew Mia had never ridden a school bus in her life other than on field trips, so this would be great news for her. Part of her nanny's duties had included taking Mia to and from her private school throughout the year.

"It'll be okay, you know." Beau squeezed the hand he was still holding.

"Eventually. I just want it to be over." Evie released a sigh.

Before Beau could respond, Mia came

bounding from the barn, Harvey at her heels. "Evie, can I start riding lessons?"

Evie's mind was on such a different plane it took her a moment to process what she was asking. "What? Today?"

Mia shook her head and laughed. "No, silly. Next week. When I start school."

Evie's heart jumped into her throat. "Actually… I need to talk to you about some things. How do you feel about staying with Norah for a little while? Just until we can make sure things are safe again here."

Mia shrugged. "That works for me."

Her sister was always so nonchalant about things. Evie had expected her to be happy, excited, even. "It may be for a couple of weeks."

"Fine," Mia said. "So I guess I can't start learning to ride until after that?"

Evie looked to Beau for help. He shrugged.

"Mia, let's worry about riding lessons later, okay? There are more important things to worry about right now. I promise you can start as soon as it becomes possible." Evie stood and walked over to her sister. She folded her into a hug.

Mia hugged her back, reluctantly at first, then seemed to realize something was different. "This is a big deal, huh?"

Evie looked down at her and nodded. "I'll

explain everything later tonight. Go on and start packing your things."

But the ranch remained quiet, even a while after Mia had gone to stay with the Sharums. The days passed in slow anticipation of a dreaded event that never came. The FBI came and questioned Evie and sent protection for her, and with so many people standing guard around her and nothing happening, she began to wonder if White had given up.

After a couple of days, Evie agreed to let Whitney start teaching Mia to ride while she was staying with the Sharums, and she called daily to report on how things were going. Whitney told Evie that Mia was doing fantastic, and Mia was so excited she practically bubbled over every time she talked about riding. Evie hated that she was missing such a big thing in her sister's life, but it couldn't be helped.

At the end of the second full week with no attacks or threats, she begged Beau to let her start working on her property. Her leg had fully healed, and she was caught up on everything Beau needed her to complete around the ranch house except for daily meals.

"I don't have enough to do, and I really need something to keep my mind occupied." Evie stood her ground when he protested.

Beau was reluctant, but he finally agreed to let her pick some colors and start painting the walls at her house. The hands had helped him repair the roof and new shingles were in place, the windows were currently being replaced and the plumbing was almost done. She wanted to paint the kitchen cabinets and replace the countertops as well, so they made a trip to the home improvement store. When they had picked out what she wanted and had it delivered, there was still no cause for alarm. Beau, too, began to wonder aloud if White had given up.

They began to prepare the house for the cosmetic renovations, taping and priming the walls and cabinets, and Beau stayed close by throughout the time she worked. They kept close watch, and one of the bodyguards from a local civilian agency the FBI had sent kept a vigilant patrol on the county road outside Evie's property.

On the third afternoon while they were working, Beau got a call from Payne that they had an emergency at the barn. One of the hands had been kicked by a horse, and they were afraid he might need to go to the hospital.

"Go on." Evie motioned him out. "There's been no cause for concern in over two weeks, and the guard is out there patrolling. I'll be fine until you get back."

Beau frowned. "I'll only be gone a few minutes. If it's bad, I'll either call an ambulance or have one of the other hands drive him to the hospital."

"I'll be just fine. I'll lock the doors and probably never know you're gone." Evie smiled.

He finally agreed to go, albeit reluctantly, and Evie kept on painting. She had to stop every so often and rest her arms, for the rollers were starting to make her ache after so many hours of repetitive movement. Deciding to take a break, she settled herself by a large window in the rear of the house where she had a built-in cushioned window seat. It was roomy and so comfortable she didn't want to get up. She hadn't slept well in a long time, and it was certainly catching up with her. She closed her eyes for a moment to enjoy it.

The next thing she knew, she was waking up in a haze.

She sat up, sniffing the strange smell and trying to shake off the disoriented fog that accompanied deep sleep. When it finally registered to her what had awakened her, a deep panic sent her adrenaline into a surge.

Her house wasn't just looking hazy from her nap. It was full of smoke.

* * *

Beau bit back his frustration.

Not only had Sawyer been kicked in the head, but he had also been stepped on. And to make matters worse, it sounded as if it was his own foolishness that had caused it. He needed stitches, a CT scan in case of concussion and X-rays to rule out broken ribs. But he wasn't cooperating with the other men even though they were all telling him he needed to go to the hospital. By the time they had him convinced, Beau realized it had been much longer than he had meant to be away from Evie.

He waved Sawyer and Payne down the driveway and was about to get in his truck when his phone rang. When he saw it was from the guard watching Evie's house, his heart rate kicked up. He had called the guy to let him know he had an emergency to deal with at the ranch and was leaving Evie there to continue painting for a little bit.

"Beau Thorpe." He answered in a businesslike tone.

"Mr. Thorpe, this is Officer Lansing. I'm on the far edge of my patrol and just heard an explosion coming from somewhere near Ms. Langston's house. I can see smoke and believe her house is on fire." He was speaking quickly, and it sounded like he was running.

"I'm on my way." Beau tried not to shout. He wanted to slam his hands against the steering wheel, but it would only waste time. How could they have known his guard was down for such a short time? Evie's attackers had taken the smallest window of opportunity and turned it to their advantage. Was it White? Were they ready for him if it was?

He drove as fast as safety would allow, and when he got there, the house was already in flames. He jumped out and ran toward the door.

The bodyguard was right behind him. "I've already called the fire department. I looked in all the windows, but I couldn't see her. They should be here with trucks and gear soon."

Beau glanced at him and gave a nod. "That's all well and good, but I'm not waiting."

The man looked at Beau in shock as he pulled up the collar of his button-down shirt and covered his nose with it. He was going to have to push his way in the door by force if she had locked it like she had promised. He might have tools in his truck that would help, but he didn't have time to dig them out.

A couple of well-placed kicks had the door splintering. Once the heat from the hungry fire subsided, he reached in and twisted the lock, swinging what was left of the door open. He began yelling for Evie, but the only answer was a cough somewhere in the back of the house. He followed the sound, crouching low and rushing through the smoke and flames.

He found her lying in a heap near the back door. He scooped her up and ran out the back with her. They had barely cleared the door when the airflow created a great resurgence in the fire and it flared with renewed fervor, billowing around them. He dived for the ground, rolling with her to protect her from major injury.

The jolt brought her around. Her eyes fluttered open. "Beau?"

"Don't talk. You're going to need to be treated for smoke inhalation." He shushed her.

"Tried to get out." She rolled the rest of the way over onto her back, then looked up at him.

"I shouldn't have left you. The men should've taken care of it without me." He felt anger and frustration sending blood pulsing through his head. "That was a dumb risk I shouldn't have taken."

She was shaking her head.

"No. Don't talk. You can argue with me later." Beau laid a finger to her lips.

She tried to smile, but it was weak from her predicament. The bodyguard came sprinting around the house then.

"I'm so glad you found her." He was breathing heavily. "There's an ambulance on the way."

He filled Beau in on his side of the story again, and Evie listened intently. The fact that he felt the need to repeat the story to Beau made him appear a little suspicious, though. Had he somehow been lax in his duties? Accidentally fallen asleep? Or was it something worse?

Beau hated to be suspicious of anyone in law enforcement, but it was odd that nothing had happened in so many days since the FBI had sent guards to patrol, but the one time Beau had called and said he wouldn't be right there with Evie, her house had caught fire, and apparently there had been some kind of small explosion to start the fire.

Beau did his best to hide his suspicions from the other man. He was looking at Beau right now. But he would definitely be watching this guy. It was an awfully big coincidence where Beau was concerned.

Paramedics treated Evie, and firefighters had the blaze under control in minutes. The damage seemed to be confined to the north end of the house, saving it from being a total loss. He made a mental note to send Payne out to take a general assessment of the damage first thing the next morning when the embers had cooled a bit more.

For the time being, he walked around the exterior, taking in what damage he could to be able to give Evie an honest report later on when she began to ask about it. He knew she would.

His heart ached for her. It seemed she was suffering from one heartbreak after another lately. He wanted nothing more than to make all her heartache and suffering go away.

The house was brick, so the outside hadn't taken much damage other than the door he had busted in. He thought it would improve the look of the place to have a new front door anyway, and he vowed to buy her the best one he could find to replace it. She would protest, but he didn't mind. The windows might need a good cleaning, and it would take some time to air out the smoke, but it shouldn't be too difficult to make it livable.

She was watching him from the gurney when he rounded the corner of the house to see how she was faring. The troubled look in her eyes made him want to fold her into his arms and keep her there, safe. He approached her with a gentle greeting.

"Feeling better?" He pointed at his throat.

She nodded. "Still a little sore."

“You’ll be sore for a few days, for sure.” The female paramedic tilted her head at her. “You would have been in much worse shape had this gentleman not gotten you out when he did.”

She didn’t elaborate, just gave Beau a pat on the shoulder and moved to the front of the truck.

“She said I was off the hook as soon as I’ve had enough oxygen.” Evie pointed at the mask.

“Good. I’m sure you’re ready to clean up and settle in for the evening.” Even as he said so, the sky seemed to darken a shade as the sun sank a bit lower.

The smell of the smoke mingled with the smell of leaves and woodsmoke that seemed to linger in the air. Fall had a smell, and it was here. He checked his watch and realized the shortening daylight hours were another hint at the change of seasons. Even so, it was past the dinner hour.

“Let me take care of getting us some food for tonight. I told Payne to get pizza for the guys with everything going on. I’ll get us some takeout from somewhere in town, and we can relax the rest of the night.”

Evie nodded. He knew she was probably too tense once more to relax, but she wouldn’t want to tell him that. “What about the fire? Obviously someone started it if the officer heard an explosion. But how did he get in and out unseen?"

Beau could feel the lines of his face deepen. "We'll talk about that later."

She seemed to understand, for she looked around at all the other people still within hearing distance. "Okay."

There were a great many things he wanted to talk to her about later. He just didn't know how he would ever be able to reconcile some of them with what he truly wanted.

SEVENTEEN

Disheartened didn't even begin to describe how Evie was feeling. She wanted nothing more than to make this whole thing with Rich White and Ruark's murder go away. If she hadn't been foolish enough to get involved with a man like Ruark in the first place, maybe this wouldn't be happening right now.

As smoke continued to waft skyward and smoldering embers sparkled like orange glitter around the rubble from the kitchen and living room, where the fire had been extinguished, Evie felt as though the house mocked her. She was at such a loss. Maybe she had taken on more than she could do, a woman alone trying to raise her younger sister. Perhaps her dream of opening a therapy center should have waited. Her sister should have come first and creating a stable home for Mia was more important than opening a therapy center.

She turned away, vowing not to dwell on

her losses tonight. There would be plenty of time to fret over this tomorrow. She was far too weary to waste concern over it right then.

Once they were back at the Thorpe ranch, Evie went up to try to wash away the smoke smell. After showering, she found Beau in the kitchen setting takeout fried rice and egg rolls on the table. He had even fixed her a glass of soda with light ice, just as she always made it for herself. The fact that he had noticed her habits made her insides go a little soft and warm.

"I hope Cho's is okay with you. I didn't think to ask before you disappeared upstairs." Beau glanced up at her through his lowered brows as he settled silverware alongside the chopsticks. He preferred to eat his Chinese food with a knife and fork, but he had seen Evie use chopsticks for hers. His hair was getting longer, and a thick, wavy lock fell over his forehead, making him look dashing and dangerous.

She should heed that mental warning instead of staring while her heart fluttered like a schoolgirl's.

"That's perfect." She smiled, unable to temper the softening of her features along with her insides.

"I heard back from Foster Golding while you were upstairs. The footage was all the same from your bank. Whoever the woman was, she was very careful not to show her face to the cameras." Beau was adjusting everything on the table to prepare for their meal.

"Of course. I expected as much." She just shrugged.

They sat down to eat, but suddenly she wasn't all that hungry. After the events of the day, she wasn't sure why she was feeling so affected by his nearness, the masculine smell of his hair gel mixed with a leather and denim scent that was signature Beau. It made her want to spend every evening sitting across from him for the rest of her life.

His eyes met hers and held. Neither spoke for a moment, but a small ding from Beau's cell phone broke their connection. He pulled his eyes from her face and picked up the phone.

"It's from Dean." His brow furrowed as he opened and read the message.

"Is everything okay?" Evie looked down at her chopsticks for a second to clear her head.

"We were both a little suspicious of the fire happening in that small window of time while I was away from you checking on Sawyer. So Dean spoke to the officer who was supposed to be keeping watch. It seems he's confessed to taking a bribe from one of White's men to let them know if I left you alone for any amount of time at the house." He looked angry, and she felt her own fury welling up inside.

"How could he do such a thing?" Evie's eyes filled with tears.

"People will do a lot of things for money, unfortunately." Beau looked like he was fighting his own anger as well.

"It can't be helped. Don't blame yourself." Evie set her chopsticks down and gave him a long look before taking a drink.

"I can't help it. I should've just had the men deal with it. Or taken you with me. Instead, I trusted the guy to guard the property and watch over you." He just shook his head.

She didn't know what more to say. They finished eating without much further discussion. Beau cleaned up from their takeout, and they moved into the living room to watch a movie. While they searched, Beau made small talk.

"What can we do to help keep your mind off things until we can wrap this up?" he finally asked.

Evie didn't even hesitate. "I'd like to see Mia."

Beau blew out a breath. "I was afraid you might say that. We will try to go see her tomorrow then. Maybe just for a short visit, though."

It didn't happen, however. An early season ice storm blew in early the next morning. The weather forecast had only given a slight chance, and though it would likely warm up later in the day and melt it off, Beau didn't want to take the chance.

They made hot chocolate and stayed inside instead.

"So the paramedic mentioned some interesting things about your brothers. Apparently you're the only one still single?" She lowered her lashes.

"It would seem so. Did she also tell you Caldwell doesn't consider himself a part of the family anymore? None of us have ever met his wife." Beau ran a hand through his wavy hair.

"She mentioned that things were different with Caldwell." Evie didn't really know how to put it. She didn't want to offend him by saying something wrong.

"We've tried everything. But he and Avery got into it over our mother one night, and he never came back around. She left us all with our father when we were young and didn't come back for years. Most of us extended forgiveness once she explained her reasons. It still hurt, but we were willing to accept that she was repentant. Not Caldwell. He still wants nothing to do with her."

"I'm sorry to hear that. I hope he eventually comes around." Evie truly meant it.

"Me, too. It's going to destroy him if he

doesn't let it go." Beau leaned into her, and she felt warmth permeating her form despite the chill of the day.

"It's probably safe to go check on that foal if you'd like to come with me. I doubt anyone is out in this weather. He might need a little extra attention, though, since it's cold." Beau stood and offered her his hand.

She took it and felt the tingle spread clear to her toes.

His warm expression made her forget all about the icy weather outside. Instead, she was wondering how she was ever going to go back to living every day without him.

Beau watched Evie's face light up as they worked with the foal. He was feisty, but she soon had him nuzzling her and following her around the corral.

They had blanketed him and taken him out of the stall to get some fresh air, and he wasted no time at all romping and acting silly. It was all the confirmation Beau needed that he was feeling much better.

"We'll go ahead and keep giving him antibiotics to make sure he doesn't have a relapse, but he seems back to himself today." Beau grinned at the colt's antics.

"He does seem to have recovered quickly."

Evie stood very still while he sniffed at her hand and nosed around for a treat.

Beau pulled one out of his pocket and handed it to her to give him. "He's about eight months old. Just past weaning age. He didn't do well with weaning."

"Poor guy." She offered him the treat and laughed as he gobbled it up. "Do you always carry treats around?"

His sheepish expression answered her question. "It's a habit I've had since my teens."

"Cute." Evie gave him a playful grin.

He merely returned her smile.

The wind gusted from time to time, but the sun came out as the afternoon progressed. Dean checked in later in the evening, and though Evie was still hoping to go to see Mia soon, the best she could do for the time being was talk to her via FaceTime.

Beau helped her with dinner for the hands that evening. They put together a hearty stew and sweet cornbread that the ranch hands devoured after the cold fall day. Afterward as they were cleaning up, Beau asked Evie about her therapy center.

"What made you want to open an equine rehabilitation center?" He was loading rinsed bowls into the dishwasher and didn't look up until Evie didn't answer right away.

"I haven't really told anyone this story." She wiped her hands on a dish towel and stepped back as Beau rinsed out the sink.

"Is it something you'd rather not talk about?" He did look at her face then, his eyes roaming over it as if to see if there was a clue there as to her thoughts.

"No." She paused again. "It would probably be best if I did talk about it."

Beau offered her a chair at the kitchen table. She sat and he waited until she began to speak, slowly at first.

"My grandfather wasn't in my life for a long time, but I thought he was a brilliant, amazing man. We had a special relationship, and he used to tell me lots of stories." She paused, probably deciding how to proceed, he thought. "He fought in the Vietnam War with the army. When I was old enough to understand, he told me stories about it. He never went into graphic detail, but he told me enough that I understood he had seen some terrible things. It was obviously painful for him, but he seemed to feel better after talking about it. However, he had a friend from the war who had no outlet for his traumatic memories. He was diagnosed with PTSD and eventually committed suicide. It devastated my grandfather, and he often spoke to me about wishing he could have done something to help his friend. When I studied similar things as I worked toward my college degree, I remembered how much my grandfather wanted to help. It made me want to help, too. It was one thing I could do for my grandfather, even now that he's gone."

Her eyes misted and he reached for her. "I understand what that's like. I'm glad you're doing something to help."

She leaned into his shoulder as he pulled her into his arms. "I'm sure you've seen a lot of terrible things as well. Maybe it seems silly to you."

He shook his head. "Not at all. I know a lot of men who could benefit from accepting some help. I struggled for a long time myself. But family and ranch responsibilities helped pull me through. Not everyone has that. I'm so glad your grandfather had you."

"So am I. And I'm very glad you were able to get past your trauma as well. I might not be here now if not for you." She pulled back and looked into his eyes.

He saw so much emotion there it frightened him. But at the same time, he couldn't look away.

He had certainly gotten himself into a mess.

He just wasn't sure it was something he wanted to escape.

EIGHTEEN

Evie's cell phone rang, interrupting the moment. Realizing it was Whitney, she answered it right away. Mia might need something.

"Evie, I'm sorry to bother you, but it's Mia. We can't find her. The girls were out playing in the pasture and Norah said they decided to play hide-and-seek around the caves, but now we can't find her." Whitney's voice sounded panic-stricken.

Evie had answered Whitney's call on speaker, so when her eyes met Beau's, she could see her worry reflected in his face.

"The caves around the bluffs?" Beau's question sent even more fear spiraling through Evie.

"The very ones. We've warned Norah not to play around there without adults close by, but I suppose she wanted to show them off to her new friend. You know how kids can be about such things." Whitney's voice was full of apology.

"Yes, I'm afraid so. Listen, we're on our way. Could you get a couple of good horses saddled for Evie and me? I think horses will be our best bet around the caves and bluffs. ATVs wouldn't maneuver as well." Beau had already motioned Evie toward the door and followed her out.

"Absolutely. Dean and I will go as well. I'll get my mom to come stay with Norah." Whitney disconnected and Evie did the same.

Nausea filled Evie as she considered all the possibilities. She prayed fervently that Mia would be found safely and protected from harm until she was found. The sun was falling low on the horizon already and searching in the dark would be tough, not to mention the temperatures would dip dramatically after sunset.

The scent of dust from passing cars mingled with the autumn woodsmoke swirling among the scattering of ranch houses and barns.

They were heading toward the Sharum ranch before Beau spoke up from behind the wheel. "We'll find her, Evie. Don't let the fear overwhelm you."

He reached across the center console and grasped her hand.

"I should have let her take Harvey. I just didn't want to put any added burden on Whitney and Dean. Harvey always looks after Mia, though." Evie was still watching the sky. A few low clouds were rolling in, and the air smelled a little like rain. She was glad the temperatures had warmed considerably. Another round of ice didn't appeal to her at all. The wind was moving the leaves on the trees along the side of the road, and she could imagine the sound of air rustling the vibrant fall-colored leaves. She hadn't even yet taken the time to appreciate the beauty of the changing season. The weeks had slid by almost unnoticed because of her anxiety.

Beau's soothing voice brought her back to the situation at hand. "You didn't expect her to need looking after. It could be she's just wandered too far and gotten lost. She's not accustomed to Wyoming."

"True. She isn't used to being out in the country at all." Evie chewed her bottom lip with one side of her front teeth.

"Dean will make sure a search and rescue dog is brought in if we don't find her soon." Beau squeezed her hand.

Once they reached the Sharum ranch, Beau

drove right out to the barn. Dean and Whitney were waiting for them just outside, holding the reins of four horses. They both wore worried expressions, and Whitney began to apologize again as soon as Evie got out of Beau's truck.

Evie shook her head. "These things happen. I just hope White hasn't found a way to get to her. But I certainly don't blame you."

After a short briefing on how they planned to search, the four of them mounted the horses, almost a matched set of beautiful dark bays. Evie settled into the saddle with a small sigh. If it weren't such a disconcerting situation, she would be thrilled to be on horseback once more. It had been several long months since she had been able to ride. As it was, she knew she wouldn't be able to enjoy it because of her fear for Mia.

They rode out at a brisk pace, forcing Evie to recall her horsemanship skills immediately. She followed behind Beau, grateful he wasn't witnessing her jolting reminders to balance and center herself in the saddle. One of Whitney's old saddles fit her well, however, so it didn't take her long to get comfortable riding again.

Dean led the way atop the largest of the dark bay horses, and once they reached the caves, they split off in different directions, Beau and

Evie taking the side of the ranch where the steep bluffs would soon begin to interrupt the landscape. The horses picked their way along carefully, their hooves clicking daintily against the occasionally rocky outcropping.

The sun was sinking quickly as they called out Mia's name repeatedly, leaving a fiery red and gold autumn sunset in its wake. No answer to their calls came, and while they saw a few small footprints in some of the dustier areas, no trail was distinct enough to follow. After what seemed an eternity to Evie at this pace, Beau motioned for her to stop her horse.

"We need to start searching in the caves. We're losing light and warmth quickly, and we don't dare delay any longer. I think the best thing to do is to stay together, though. There is no telling what might be taking shelter in the caves, and I don't want you to meet up with a bear or mountain lion alone." Beau's wince indicated he didn't relish having to bring up such things.

He began to dismount, and she followed suit, leaving the horses to graze around the edge of the rocky caves, reins dangling.

Evie fought to maintain a neutral expression. Whatever might be inside the caves, her sister needed help. "Should I lead or follow?"

"You can follow." Beau had had the foresight to bring a flashlight, and he turned it on as he stepped into the first cave. It was barely large enough for them to stand up inside, and a quick sweep confirmed it was empty.

They continued on like this through a few more caves, neither saying much to the other as the daylight outside the orifices waned with increasing speed. Urgency spurred Evie past her frustration, fueling her determination to find her sister.

By the time they reached the last of the caves, Evie was calling Mia's name once more. A quick text to Dean confirmed they weren't finding any more promising clues to Mia's location than Evie and Beau were. Fatigue began to weigh on Evie, counterbalanced with the last vestiges of adrenaline her body was able to produce after over an hour of searching. She sat down on a rock, not realizing it was the edge of one of the smaller bluffs.

"Evie, be careful." Beau's voice was edged with raw frustration. "We can't have you falling off a ledge and getting hurt right now."

She jumped to her feet. "Oh, I'm sorry. I didn't realize..."

Beau looked at her for a long moment. He doubtless saw the haggard lines of her weariness etched across her face. Her self-talk was weakening. No amount of reassurance was helping. She began to pray silently once more.

Lord, please help us find her. Show us where she is. Give us something, please.

"Can you manage one more cave? This one is quite a bit larger than any of the others. I'd let you stay here and rest, but I don't know how long it will take." Beau's own face bore signs of disillusionment as well. If he was giving up on finding Mia, what did that say? Was their cause lost?

Evie wouldn't let the negative thoughts take root. She took a deep breath and stepped toward him. "I'm right behind you."

The last cave extended far back into the side of a mountain, just as Beau had promised, and while they had yet to encounter any wild creature fiercer than a bat, Evie clamped her jaws and stepped gingerly across the dirt floor. About halfway through, Beau stopped.

"What is it?" Evie questioned.

He stooped and picked something up. "This isn't Mia's, but someone has been here."

Evie drew closer and saw that he held a dark stocking cap in his hand. Shining the flashlight at the floor of the cave, Beau's light illuminated scuffs and wrinkles in the soft dirt as if someone had been lying on the floor there. Someone had been taking shelter here.

"Why would anyone be hiding out in this cave?" Evie's voice shook. She thought she knew the answer. This would be a good lookout point for someone trying to observe the comings and goings at the ranch. The reason things had been so quiet lately became suddenly clear. Rich White had devised another plan to get to Evie. He had kidnapped Mia.

Beau's response was to hurry to the mouth of the cave and send a text to Dean. Was he drawing the same conclusion?

She followed him, her mind churning. A black toboggan wasn't all that unusual in the cold evenings in Wyoming, but this cave was so far away from anything, it didn't make sense for someone to just be out here lounging around. From the mouth of the cave, she could see the Sharum's ranch house sitting down in the valley, the barns and yard clearly visible on this slight rise.

She shivered as the night air swirled around her, the dusk now deepening into purple night. Where had he taken Mia? Her chest seized up violently, an ache piercing through her whole chest cavity as she tried to just breathe. Her brave little sister… Evie only hoped Mia didn't try anything foolish before they could find her.

A moment later, she heard Beau talking on the phone, and he turned away to look off in the direction Dean and Whitney had taken. The horses stomped and snorted in their impatience to get back to the barn for their evening meal, and Evie never heard a sound behind her until a hand snaked around her mouth and a low voice whispered in her ear.

"Don't scream. Don't make a sound." The cold nose of a pistol grazed her temple, and she shook with the effort not to cry out in terror.

The arm started tugging her backward toward the cave, and panic seized her. She struggled, but only for a moment as the muzzle of the pistol thumped heartily against her temple as a reminder.

They had almost reached the mouth of the cave once more when Beau turned and saw what was happening.

"Evie!" He cried out her name and then rapidly told Dean she had a gun to her head, and they needed help.

The phone dropped to the ground as the arm yanked her forcefully into the cave. Beau lunged toward them, but the voice shouted a warning.

"Don't come any closer or I'll shoot her. That's the goal, anyway." The words came out with an evil sneer.

"Let her go. The others will be here any

minute and then you're out of options." Beau tried to talk him down.

"Oh? It seems I'm the one with all the options right now. I'm the man holding the gun."

Beau couldn't really argue the point. He groaned angrily but stood where he was. "What are you going to do? When you come out of the cave, and eventually you'll have to come out, we'll be waiting for you."

"You see, that's where my plan is solid. This cave has an exit on the other side. Before anyone can ride all the way around and find where the cave exits on the back side, we will have made it through the cave and escaped." The man's voice took on a manic tone. He was trying to talk in a falsetto, but Beau was pretty sure this was Rich White himself. The discarded cap must have belonged to someone else, though, because White was wearing one that bore a strong resemblance to the one Beau had found in the cave, only this one extended over most of his face like a ski mask.

"Come on, White. The Feds are after you. You're just adding to your sentence at this point." Beau felt a reckless urge to call his bluff.

"That may be true, but they won't have her as a witness. That might make it a little harder to convict me of murder." He didn't try to continue with the terrible falsetto after that. "And you didn't actually see me kidnap her or her sister."

Beau couldn't believe the man's bravado. "They'll just find something else to convict you with. It isn't like your list of crimes is short. And you got careless over Evie's alibi. Who's to say you won't mess up again?"

"That wasn't my fault." He snorted. "It doesn't matter, anyway. She should've just gone to prison—better than being dead."

Beau needed to keep him talking to give Dean time to get there. "That's a little unnecessary, isn't it? Just because she ruined your plan?"

"Yeah, but now I'm angry about it. Look, love to stay and chat, but we have things to do, right, sweetheart?" He seemed to be catching on. He aimed his pistol at Beau and fired off a shot just as Beau dove for cover. Evie almost wrenched away, while the gun was pointed elsewhere, though, so he focused on her again.

"I'll deal with you later." White called out the words in a frustrated voice. Things didn't seem to be going as the criminal had hoped.

White ducked into the cave, dragging Evie along. Beau couldn't hold in the groan of frustration. He waited until they were out of sight, and then followed very carefully. If White knew he was there, no telling what he would try.

He didn't turn on his flashlight since it would quickly alert White to his presence. Instead, he felt his way carefully along the walls of the cave as he maneuvered the space. He could hear White clumsily dragging Evie along, as he had no hand available with which to hold a flashlight. As the darkness of the cavern became oppressive, he heard White tell Evie to turn on the light on her phone and hold it out for them. She didn't answer at all, but soon a thin shaft of light illuminated the interior of the cave ahead. Beau shrank back against the wall, sure that White would notice him now that there was some light. Evidently he didn't expect Beau to follow, though, for he simply trudged on with Evie without looking back. Evie, however, glanced over her shoulder as White guided her around a corner. Her eyes flickered for a split second, but to her credit, she never let on that she had seen anything.

Beau waited a few beats to be sure his nemesis wouldn't change his mind and turn for a look, but then he slowly crept along behind them. He called up from his memory every stealthy move he had learned as a ranger. The cave stretched on, even farther than Beau thought it did. Finally, a sliver of light became visible in the distance. It would have been easy to miss if White hadn't told him where it was, almost like a trick of the mind, or perhaps a little bit of light shining in from a crack over head in the top of the cave. But closer study revealed it was a slight opening between jutting rocks where they overlapped and tumbled over one another. It looked like an earthquake or avalanche had stacked the rocks haphazardly around the crevice, leaving a bit of a maze to the exit. But the fact remained that an opening was there, however obscure.

Beau shrank down as White approached the opening with Evie in tow. He wanted to see how he managed this. It didn't look large enough for Evie's small frame to squeeze through, much less White's much larger form.

Beau could just barely make out White's words to Evie as they paused before the rubble.

"You first." White shoved Evie toward the pile of boulders, aiming the gun at her.

Beau could barely make out Evie's petite form trying to maneuver in, over, under and around the odd shapes to get through the hole. He couldn't see much past the first few rocks, and she disappeared into them. When she seemed to have made it far enough that White's gun couldn't reach her, Beau took a chance.

"Stop right there!" He held his own gun, pointed at White. The sliver of light provided just enough relief from the dark to make Beau's shadow visible against the light winking off his Glock.

White turned with a roar of anger.

"Evie, if you can hear me, run!"

NINETEEN

Evie heard Beau's voice call out from the cave just behind Rich White's roar of outrage. She scrambled the last few inches out of the hole, legs first, and lit out as fast as she could move across the rocky landscape. It was a long way back around to the horses, and she needed to take cover until Beau had things under control. There had to be somewhere to hide. She couldn't help Mia if she was captured before she could get to her.

She considered the other caves, but they were equally distant, and they would likely be one of the first places White looked if he got away before Beau could restrain him. She needed a better plan.

She kept moving until she found an outcropping she could duck beneath, and she paused to catch her breath, keeping watch for either of the men to emerge. She had thought she heard the sounds of a scuffle as she darted away, but she expected at least one of them to come out of the opening soon.

She called Whitney and quietly told her what had happened, and Whitney promised Dean was already on his way and she would be right behind him. Once she disconnected, she went back to keeping watch. It seemed like far too many minutes had passed and she still hadn't seen anyone. Was Beau going to be able to get to her?

Her heart hammered and she breathed deeply, trying to calm herself. She needed something to do, an action to take. She started moving, staying low against the outcropping, until her feet felt a give in the earth. Looking up a little way, she could see one of the bluffs Beau had spoken about dropping off not far ahead.

She would just have to stay put.

A grunt alerted her attention back to the exit of the cave. She crouched as low as she could and peeked around the outcropping. It was Rich White. Her hopes fell.

His nose and forehead were bleeding, and he looked like he had taken a few punches, but he was scanning the area looking for her. How had he possibly bested Beau? She couldn't believe it. And most of all, was he okay? She prayed White hadn't killed him.

Evie ducked back behind the rock to try to

figure out what to do. She began to pray silently once more. She needed Dean to get there quickly. If she had to move, White would see her immediately.

She stayed as still as she possibly could, listening for any warning of his approach. His feet scuffled against the rocks and dirt, but he didn't seem to be getting much closer. Where was Dean? They must have ridden far off in the opposite direction.

She tried to scoot silently around to see if she could somehow get farther from White, even if she had to take the long way around the bluff. She might have to get closer to him before she could get farther away.

She eased around, trying to be quiet, but she took too long deciding. She heard him creeping close and her heart hammered. She closed her eyes as she sensed his approach on the other side of the outcropping. She sent up a fervent prayer for protection.

"Oh, you can't get away that easily."

When she looked up, White was standing above her on the rock, smirking down at her. Her heart nearly stopped, and then resumed its pounding with a renewed urgency.

"Where is my sister!" She was tired of playing his games. "I don't care what happens to me, but I want to see my sister safe."

He chuckled. "Your sister is safely tucked into an old farmhouse nearby. But you won't be seeing her again."

"Why did you have someone put the money in my account? Why did you keep asking me for your money if you put it there in the first place?" Evie wanted answers. If she was to die, she wanted to know why he was doing all this.

He laughed. "You see, that's the funny part. It was your dear old Ruark who found your stunt double and had the money put in your account. Oh, yes. I have seen the footage. I have friends in high places." He paused a second, and she blew out a breath of surprise. "It did give me the means to make you look guilty, though. It would have worked out much better if your darling boyfriend hadn't had so much faith in you, though. He should have abandoned you instead of hiding the money with you."

Evie squeezed her eyes shut. Ruark had done this to her? Provided a means for her to be framed for his murder and hidden the money away in her account? He was even more despicable than she had ever imagined.

White drew her attention back to himself now, however. He scrambled down the side of the rock face to where she was. He didn't look behind him, and she didn't know if he realized how close to the precipice he was. "I've had enough of you and your new boyfriend. Time's up for you."

"I don't know about that."

Beau's voice sent hope soaring through Evie. He was already on the other side of the rock, where he had made his way down and around silently. Evie wanted nothing more than to throw her arms around him at that moment.

"I left you unconscious in the cave." White looked furious. "How?"

Beau shrugged. "Survival skills."

Then he lunged at White.

The two men rolled around on the ground, alternately throwing punches, until Beau finally landed a good solid punch to White's midsection, sending him sprawling and gasping for air.

But he had also rolled closer to the edge of the bluff.

Beau took a moment to catch his breath, sucking in air to counteract the exertion he had just put forth until White began to squirm with the apparent intent to come after him once more.

Both men had lost their weapons in the struggle, and Evie realized that Beau's Glock was close enough that she might be able to reach it. Rich White's Ruger, however, had skidded over a few rocks and slipped out of sight. White began to wriggle his way toward where he had last seen it, inching himself closer to the edge he apparently still hadn't noticed was a steep drop-off. His attention was on the gun.

Beau took advantage of White's distraction and made a move then. He kicked at White's hand as he reached toward the Ruger. While Beau had his adversary occupied, Evie lurched for Beau's Glock. Before she could get to it, however, a gasp drew her attention back to where the men were still scrambling for the upper hand. White had wrenched Beau closer and was now trying to push him over the edge of the bluff. White's face was red from the exertion, and Evie felt a skitter in her pulse before it raced ahead. Beau wasn't that easily outmaneuvered, however, and as Evie reached the gun and rose to attempt to halt White's efforts, a grunt and sliding rock sounded just before White's scream. Evie watched as he overreacted to Beau's counterattack, losing his balance, and slipping slowly over the edge.

Beau threw out a hand in a last-ditch effort to catch him, but it was too late.

A horrible scream echoed through the hills as White slid off the bluff. Beau scrambled to his feet and went to look over. He closed his eyes.

"Is he..." Evie couldn't quite make herself finish. That could have been Beau. She couldn't stand the thought. It made her chest ache and her eyes water.

"I don't know but if he's not, he's not going to be in very good condition. Call an ambulance." Beau didn't give her any time to do so, though. His long legs covered the distance between them in a few short strides, and he had her in his arms before she could even think about pulling out her phone.

He gently took the Glock from her as she stood staring in shock.

"Beau, that could have been you." The words came out on a sob. "I can't lose you."

He leaned back just enough to look at her. His intense expression jarred her back to him. Her heart raced for a new reason. His tender touch on her chin came just before his lips came gently down against her own. His kiss felt like coming home after a long journey, and she wanted to melt into him. She sighed against his lips, and he smiled.

"You're not going to lose me. In fact, you may never get rid of me. I love you, Evie Langston. I love you and I adore Mia, and I want us to make a home together. Can you give me a chance?" He was searching her face now, and she wondered if he could read her amazed and wonder-filled thoughts. How could this amazing man have come to love her? He was right out of her fondest dreams and more than she could have ever hoped for in a man.

"Of course I'll give you a chance. I love you, Beau Thorpe! So much you wouldn't believe it." She kissed him back then, and that's how the Sharums found them when they came riding up a few seconds later.

"Well, well," Dean Sharum teased. "Looks like things have worked out in ways I didn't expect while we were riding across the ranch."

"Oh!" Whitney threw Dean an incredulous look. "What do you mean you didn't expect this?"

They both laughed.

"Well, at least not at this moment," Dean amended his statement with a grin.

Beau pulled away then, and everyone sobered at his words. "White took a tumble off the bluff. We need an ambulance, but I'm not sure he's going to make it."

Dean dismounted and walked over to look over the edge. "It certainly doesn't look good for him."

"Has anyone found Mia? He said she's hiding out in an old farmhouse somewhere nearby." Evie was coming out from under the surprise of Beau's kiss and very anxious to find her sister.

"An old farmhouse? I think I know just

where she is. Dean, is it far to the old Graham place?" Whitney asked.

"No, it's just over that hill. Stay here with White until first responders get here. Beau and I'll go get her. Did he mention if someone is guarding her?" Dean directed this last question at Evie.

"He didn't say. Can I go?" She was already trying to gauge how far it was to her horse or if she needed to just go on foot.

Dean nodded. "I wouldn't try to keep you from it."

"Here, you and Beau can take my horse. Blitz doesn't mind the extra weight of a double rider." Whitney was already dismounting.

"Thanks." Beau took the reins and handed her his Glock. "Just in case anyone besides first responders should happen to show up."

Whitney nodded and watched them mount up and ride away. Evie muttered a quick prayer for her safety as they followed Dean over the hill in the deepening dusk. She hated to leave her, but she had to find Mia.

Just as Dean had said, they could see the abandoned farmhouse as soon as they crested the hill, and Evie's heartbeat sped up just a bit. Her thoughts raced ahead. Would Mia be okay? She would be scared, and maybe all alone, wondering what would happen to her. But had they truly not harmed her in any way?

The old house was graying and withered with decay, its windows dirt-encrusted and fragmented, and it looked as if a strong wind would turn it into a pile of toothpicks at any moment. If the inside was half as creepy as the exterior, Mia was probably terrified.

Dean motioned for them to wait a moment while he dismounted and moved closer. They dismounted and waited, Beau taking the reins of Dean's horse.

"Anyone here? Hands in the air and come out." Dean had his Glock out before calling out the directive, his stance defensive.

There was no response. Could they be fortunate enough to find Mia here alone without a guard? They waited, but no one emerged.

"This is Sheriff Dean Sharum. This is your last chance. I'm armed and I'm coming in." He stepped onto the porch, and it sagged and creaked in protest.

A window shattered to his right and he dropped down low, swinging his gun in that direction. "Rich White is already in custody, seriously injured, maybe even dead. Your game is up. Come out unarmed, and we will see what kind of deal we can make."

He hadn't even finished his words when a

noise at the back of the house drew their attention. A lone figure, dressed in camouflage clothing, shot across the back of what was once the yard and into some brush. Dean called out once more, but the figure didn't stop. The sheriff lit out after the man while Beau jumped between Evie and the fleeing suspect, just in case he had a weapon and decided to use it.

"Come on." As Dean pursued the camo-clad figure, Beau led Evie into the house, carefully testing the floor with each step before trusting it to their full weight.

He took up a defensive stance to protect Evie and swept the room with his flashlight before allowing her to enter the house. The cobwebs and dust clinging to every available surface reminded Evie of a scene from a scary movie, but the paint-chipped walls and rotten floorboards were all too real. She peeked cautiously out from behind Beau as he picked his way across the floor. The cold permeated the house, which was in shadows during the warmest part of the day. Drafty air met them around every corner, along with the stale, rotting smell of disuse and decay. The beam of Beau's high-powered flashlight barely pierced a hole in the deep darkness.

A faint light glowed from somewhere near the rear of the old structure, and Beau followed it, swinging the flashlight to and fro as they went.

They crept through the house, alert to any slight noise, until they reached a room in a back corner where an old kerosene lantern was lit, giving off a weak orange-yellow light. It flickered in the drafty air, and Evie wondered how the ancient thing even still worked. Judging from the broken fancy light fixtures and rusted lamps with their brightly colored cracked globes, it had once been a parlor or sitting room of some sort, used for entertaining. The carpet that had once covered the floor was rotted and worn beneath the dust and leaves that had blown in from the broken windows. In a corner stood a threadbare, dirty armchair with one broken leg, propped up on the fireplace bricks below one side. Mia was nestled in the dingy chair, looking small and bedraggled from her capture. When she saw them, her eyes lit with pure relief, and Evie ran to her, pulling the gag from her mouth before folding her into her embrace.

"Mia, are you okay?" Evie stroked her sister's hair and squeezed her tight.

"I was so scared." Mia shook with her silent sobs.

Beau eased closer. "Let's get you out of here so we can get you warmed up. You've been out here in the cold for too long."

He shrugged out of his own jacket and wrapped Mia into it as soon as they had freed her from the zip ties that had her bound. He picked her up gently, and she didn't protest. Outside they could make out Dean Sharum leading the handcuffed man in camouflage toward them through the darkness. A nearly full moon shone brightly overhead, casting a glow on the landscape.

"I hope this was the only one. No one else seemed to be around, and he was fleeing toward an old truck sitting on the outskirts of the property. It was empty, and his cell phone showed no signs he was communicating with anyone but White." Dean grasped the reins of his horse in a free hand momentarily, offering it to Evie to ride.

"What about you?" Evie asked, helping Mia into the saddle.

"I spoke to Whitney and the deputies are here. She is sending one to get the side-by-side in the barn. I'll ride back in the UTV with them." He indicated the suspect he held in front of him.

Beau mounted the other horse, and they rode at a moderate pace as Dean walked beside them, pushing the silent, angry man in cuffs just ahead of him. When they reached

Whitney and the deputies, she ran forward to hug Mia and Evie.

"I'm so glad you're both okay." Whitney gave them one last squeeze before relinquishing them.

"Do they have White in custody?" Evie couldn't relax until she knew it was truly over.

"Yes." Whitney paused. She glanced at Mia. "Paramedics have been working on him, but it doesn't look good."

Evie just nodded. She didn't want to discuss the particulars in front of Mia, and Whitney seemed to understand.

The flurry of activity continued as deputies and emergency personnel worked the scene, but Beau urged Evie and Mia into one of the SUVs the deputies had driven out into the field nearby to warm up. Whitney assured them she would see to the horses and wrap up any other details with the first responders. Evie couldn't wait to get Mia back to the house, cleaned up and in some warm pajamas.

It occurred to her then in the silence of the patrol unit that she had begun to think of Beau's ranch house as their home. It was going to be difficult to move on. Though she would still be working for him helping with meals and such until her house could be repaired, everything was about to change. It was time she started remembering that Beau wasn't hers. He might have told her he loved her, but the situation had changed. He would remember soon how he had said he didn't want a romantic relationship. He would change his mind.

Her heart ached with a sharp protest at the thought.

Maybe she should cut her losses and move back to Oklahoma. It would be easier to forget him if she moved home.

Beau couldn't get back to Evie and Mia soon enough. Wrapping up all the details with the deputies took far too long, and his patience had long since dissipated. He just wanted to take them home. By the time he got the chance, he was in a foul mood.

Evie took Mia upstairs as soon as they reached the ranch house, and he didn't see her again for half an hour. He was about to stomp up the stairs and find her when she finally emerged, looking weary and rumpled, but palpably relieved. He stood and walked over to meet her.

Evie paused, eyeing him warily. "Are you okay?"

"Fine." He realized how gruff he sounded and amended his answer. "I'm just fine. I'm glad it's over."

Evie sighed as she sat down. "Is it, for sure? Did Dean still think I might have to testify?"

Beau swallowed hard. He wasn't sure how she was going to take this news. "I didn't want to tell you before because Mia was with us. But Rich White coded before they could get him to the hospital in the ambulance. They transported him to the closest hospital, but he was pronounced dead upon arrival."

Her shoulders visibly relaxed. "Oh, that's wonderful. I mean, not that he's dead, but I'm so glad I don't have to testify."

"I understand." Beau couldn't agree more. "And the guy we caught fleeing the house has confessed to everything. He's hoping to get a deal with the DA."

"So now I can concentrate on getting my house repaired. I'm sure you won't mind us getting out of yours." She laughed but it sounded a bit strained.

"I actually kind of like having you both here. It's too quiet when it's just me." He examined her face. She wasn't looking at him. What was going on?

"I do really appreciate all you've done for Mia and me." Evie now examined her hands as if she had never really seen them before.

"Evie… Is something bothering you?" He didn't know what to do other than just ask.

Had she changed her mind? She had told him she loved him, too, but maybe she had just gotten swept up in the situation and now that she didn't need his protection anymore, maybe she just wanted to go back to avoiding relationships.

The thought made him a little angry. Mostly because it hurt.

"No. Nothing is bothering me. Why do you ask?"

He wanted to blurt out that it was obvious she was avoiding his eyes and she was acting like they had never confessed their feelings. She had kissed him back, hadn't she? Why did she act like they were mere acquaintances trying to make small talk now?

He stood up, running his hands through his hair with a sigh. "No reason. Look, you two are always welcome here. I'm going to call it a night."

He didn't know what to do other than remove himself from the situation right now. He clearly wasn't asking the right questions, but he had no idea what the questions were right now. He had to distance himself for a while and think. Maybe he could figure it out.

"Beau, wait." She stopped him with her quiet words.

He turned to look at her and found her expression looking just as lost as he was feeling. It softened his attitude considerably. "Evie, I don't want you to go. I was telling the truth when I said I loved you. I want you and Mia to stay. Forever."

Evie smiled, but then she started shaking her head. "It's just so soon. Are you sure? We've only known each other for a short time. You might decide you don't want me to stay after getting to know me better."

He tried not to laugh. "That's not going to happen. You might, however, decide you don't want to put up with me."

He settled down beside her and pulled her into his arms but kept just enough distance between them to look into her eyes. "Evie, I don't ever want to be separated from you again. We can take things slow, but I want you to be my wife. Will you give me a chance? Let me convince you to marry me?"

Evie's eyes were alight with happiness and her smile grew even larger. "Yes. I want to marry you, too, Beau Thorpe. But I think maybe I should make you work for it."

He laughed and then kissed her, gently at first, and then with more intensity. When he pulled away, he gave her a serious look, jaw set. "How am I doing so far?"

She laughed then but leaned back close.

"Not bad, but I might need a little more convincing."

"You're a stubborn lady, Evie Langston."

He was kissing her again when they heard Mia clearing her throat. "Sorry to interrupt. Does this mean we are staying?"

Evie flushed, but she looked at Beau when she answered. "Yes. We're staying forever."

EPILOGUE

Evie and Beau decided to have the wedding at Christmas time while all the family was back at the ranch for the holidays, so the day before Christmas Eve, they had spoken their vows to each other in a little country church full of tall windows with huge fluffy snowflakes falling outside. It was a magical day with Mia standing tall and proud beside her, along with her new sisters-in-law, Lauren, Madison and Brynn. Mia fell in love with Beau's nieces and began to immediately ask when Evie was going to have a baby. Beau's brothers found this hilarious and kept encouraging her by repeating her question.

Beau's youngest brother, Caldwell, surprised everyone by showing up at the last minute, but he wouldn't participate in the wedding. His demeanor was quiet and repentant, however, and they finally learned his wife wasn't with him because they had had a falling out, and he was trying very hard to get things back to normal. He wouldn't give them a lot of details, however, declaring he didn't want to ruin Beau and Evie's special day.

Christmas was a wonderful time of celebration for the whole family as well. After attending a small candlelight church service on Christmas Eve, the family gathered at the Thorpe ranch, which Evie had finally christened the Grace Valley Ranch. They learned Grayson and Lauren's daughter Riley was going to become a big sister within the next six months, and Brynn and Avery would be having a baby as well only a month or two behind them. Madison and Briggs were making wonderful parents to their new daughter, Livie Rose. She was a beautiful and happy baby, and everyone loved passing her around.

Caldwell seemed to want to repair his relationships with his brothers, but he left the day after Christmas, saying he needed to make things right with his wife, Natalie, somehow. He promised he would do his best to get her there to meet everyone soon.

Evie opened her therapy center just after New Year's Day and found it successful beyond her hopes by the end of the first month. Mia had asked to contribute, so they spoke to her father's lawyer about the money her father had left in trust for her. He agreed that it would be a viable option for her to make an investment with the funds, as long as it remained under his discretion until she came of age. He also arranged for Evie to receive funds to help support Mia, since she had been granted full custody of her. Mia had gotten so involved that Evie planned to make her a full partner when she became an adult. She had learned to ride quickly and was a natural hand with the horses, not to mention a great asset to the clients who came to the center because of her outgoing personality.

Beau spent a great deal of his time at the center as well, sharing his story in hopes that it would help others overcome the trauma they had suffered also. He told Evie frequently, however, that she was the real secret to his healing.

She agreed that he was also hers.

* * * * *

If you liked this story from Sommer Smith,
check out her previous
Love Inspired Suspense books,

Under Suspicion
Attempted Abduction
Ranch Under Siege
Wyoming Cold Case Secrets

Available now from
Love Inspired Suspense!

Find more great reads at
www.LoveInspired.com.

Dear Reader,

I hope you enjoyed Evie and Beau's story as they journeyed toward trust and true happiness. Beau just wanted to stay hidden on the family ranch and avoid the outside world, but Evie and Mia needed a hero. He couldn't help rising to the challenge. Though Evie was threatened and accused, her trust was in God. Man could do nothing against His law, and He saw to her protection, using Beau as his instrument. Her plans to begin a therapeutic riding center were delayed, but ultimately everything worked out by God's design, including finding a love they could both put their trust in. So it is in our own lives so often. I hope their story will inspire you to continue to trust in the Lord and believe in His goodness.

You can contact me through email at ssmith.kgc3@gmail.com.

Thank you for reading this story!

Blessings,
Sommer Smith

Get 3 FREE REWARDS!
We'll send you 2 FREE Books plus a FREE Mystery Gift.
MURDER IN THE FAMILY
A DIRE ISLE
FREE
Value Over
$20
THE EX-HUSBAND
KAREN HAMILTON
J.T. ELLISON
HER DARK LIES
Both the Mystery Library and Essential Suspense series feature compelling novels filled with gripping mysteries, edge-of-your-seat thrillers and heart-stopping romantic suspense stories.
YES! Please send me 2 FREE novels from the Mystery Library or Essential Suspense Collection and my FREE Gift (gift is worth about $10 retail). After receiving them, if I don't wish to receive any more books, I can return the shipping statement marked "cancel." If I don't cancel, I will receive 4 brand-new Mystery Library books every month and be billed just $6.74 each in the U.S. or $7.24 each in Canada, a savings of at least 25% off the cover price, or 4 brand-new Essential Suspense books every month and be billed just $7.49 each in the U.S. or $7.74 each in Canada, a savings of at least 17% off the cover price. It's quite a bargain! Shipping and handling is just 50¢ per book in the U.S. and $1.25 per book in Canada.* I understand that accepting the 2 free books and gift places me under no obligation to buy anything. I can always return a shipment and cancel at any time by calling the number below. The free books and gift are mine to keep no matter what I decide.
Choose one: ☐ Mystery Library (414/424 BPA GRPM) ☐ Essential Suspense (191/391 BPA GRPM) ☐ Or Try Both! (414/424 & 191/391 BPA GRRZ)
Name (please print)
Address
Apt. #
City
State/Province
Zip/Postal Code
Email: Please check this box ☐ if you would like to receive newsletters and promotional emails from Harlequin Enterprises ULC and its affiliates. You can unsubscribe anytime.
Mail to the Harlequin Reader Service:
IN U.S.A.: P.O. Box 1341, Buffalo, NY 14240-8531
IN CANADA: P.O. Box 603, Fort Erie, Ontario L2A 5X3
Want to try 2 free books from another series? Call 1-800-873-8635 or visit www.ReaderService.com.
*Terms and prices subject to change without notice. Prices do not include sales taxes, which will be charged (if applicable) based on your state or country of residence. Canadian residents will be charged applicable taxes. Offer not valid in Quebec. This offer is limited to one order per household. Books received may not be as shown. Not valid for current subscribers to the Mystery Library or Essential Suspense Collection. All orders subject to approval. Credit or debit balances in a customer's account(s) may be offset by any other outstanding balance owed by or to the customer. Please allow 4 to 6 weeks for delivery. Offer available while quantities last.
Your Privacy—Your information is being collected by Harlequin Enterprises ULC, operating as Harlequin Reader Service. For a complete summary of the information we collect, how we use this information and to whom it is disclosed, please visit our privacy notice located at corporate.harlequin.com/privacy-notice. From time to time we may also exchange your personal information with reputable third parties. If you wish to opt out of this sharing of your personal information, please visit readerservice.com/consumerschoice or call 1-800-873-8635. Notice to California Residents—Under California law, you have specific rights to control and access your data. For more information on these rights and how to exercise them, visit corporate.harlequin.com/california-privacy.
MYSSTS23